A SHOT IN THE DARK

MYDWORTH MYSTERIES #1

Neil Richards • Matthew Costello

RED DOG
UK

Originally published as an eBook edition by Bastei Lübbe AG,
Cologne, Germany, 2019.

Edited by Eleanor Abraham
Cover Design by Oliver Smyth

ISBN 978-1-913331-10-8

www.reddogpress.co.uk

A SHOT IN THE DARK

PROLOGUE

SUSSEX, ENGLAND, 1929.

LADY LAVINIA FITZHENRY turned the page of the novel she was reading – the latest from the American, Hemingway.

Always fun to read a book written by someone you've met – and even shared more than a few drinks with.

Sitting up in bed – Mydworth Manor so peaceful, the staff below all quiet – to read like this was such a pleasure.

She had brought a glass of port with her to bed – now sadly gone – and certainly it was late enough to think about turning the light off. Plenty to do in the busy days ahead, the house soon to be filled with weekend guests down from London.

Gossip. Music. Cocktails every evening before dinner. What fun!

She placed the book on her bedside table and put the light out. The bedroom now in darkness. She started to drift off, plans running through her mind.

But then...

A noise.

She opened her eyes. Another sound: *a rattle*. Not close, clearly somewhere down the wide hallway.

A SHOT IN THE DARK

A sound that, well, perhaps a door or a window might make in response to a stiff breeze. Except this was a perfectly still night. Barely a breeze.

There it was again. The rattle louder.

Lavinia had never been one to sit and wait. Her response to fear throughout her entire life had remained exactly the same.

If you are afraid of something, you face it.

She put the light on, and, in one quick move, slid out from under the covers, slipped on her dressing gown, and headed out onto the landing.

LAVINIA STOOD motionless outside her bedroom, listening. The sounds seemed to have stopped.

Slowly she moved along the dark hallway, ears straining.

Past the grand staircase that led down to the entrance, where she saw the glow of the entryway light that was kept on all evening.

Warm, yellow, reassuring.

Down the hallway, until she came to the row of bedrooms that would house all her guests in just a few days.

She stopped. There was nothing but quiet.

Clearly time to go back to bed, she thought. She turned.

There was a *crack*.

The sharp, brittle sound of something *snapping* in the room directly to her right.

Door shut. Secure – as it should be. These rooms were cleaned and prepared days ago.

Lavinia grabbed the doorknob – cold to the touch.

A twist, an audible click, the door opened – and she slowly entered the dark room.

With her eyes already adjusted to the dark, she didn't need light to see that all was in order here.

The door that led into the dressing room stood half open. She felt – the barest sense of it – a cold draught coming from the room. A chill that shouldn't be there.

Taking a deep breath, she grasped the door handle, pulled the door wide – and entered the room, to see... the window wide open.

She hurried over, ready to slam it shut, and end this late-night adventure. As she started to pull the window closed, her eyes were drawn for a second to the lawn as the moon momentarily found a gap in the clouds.

And she stopped. Frozen.

A figure was walking slowly away from the house towards the woods.

As she watched, the figure stopped. Turned.

Looked up at her...

Lavinia's heart, at peace only seconds ago, now pounded. She backed away from the window, thoughts racing, searching for explanations that did not come.

She took a deep breath – and then stepped back to the window again, eyes straining.

But the figure had gone. As if it had never been there.

And now, as she peered into the darkness, a feeling of foreboding came over her.

A feeling that this weekend wasn't going to bring fun at all...

A SHOT IN THE DARK

1.

AN ENGLISH HOMECOMING

KAT REILLY WATCHED her husband Harry shield his eyes from the morning sun as he studied the unloading process of the cross-channel ferry at Newhaven dock.

She knew him well enough to see that he was concerned.

The Pride of Sussex had berthed an hour late, and, in the frenzied hurry to turn the ship around, Kat had already seen one precious cargo slip from its net and smash on the quayside.

While the steamer belched smoke into the sky, hordes of trucks, horses and carts, and hand-barrows swarmed around the dock-side, as passengers called instructions, and customs men tried to intervene.

So much for all the English politeness and decorum she'd been expecting to see on this, her first trip to Britain!

Though, in truth, Sir Harry Mortimer seemed as ever to typify the calm, unruffled English gentleman.

Tall, slim, his black hair longer than she'd ever known it, jacket slung nonchalantly over one shoulder, white cotton shirt sporting a dashing red tie.

All he needed was a tennis racquet to complete the look.

Or should that be – a cricket bat?

He turned back to her. "Hmm… just going to have a quick word with those chaps over there. Make sure they, er…"

She grinned at that. "And how will that go?"

Harry – with one of his great smiles – nodded.

"You think they won't welcome my advice?"

"With open arms, I'm sure. That or clenched fists."

"That *is* my car they're about to drop on the quay."

"*Your* car?"

"Ah, right. Sorry – old habits. I mean *our* car. Thing is, she may not be a Bugatti, but that Alvis is damned precious to me."

"Good luck. Back in New York nobody argues with the longshoremen."

"Well, I fancy we're a tad more *civilised* over here."

"Civilised? Nine o'clock and I'm still waiting for that coffee you promised."

"How about we stop in at a local hostelry *en route* and celebrate my return to the motherland, and your first visit, with a slap-up breakfast?"

"Slap-up?"

"Forgot you don't quite speak the lingo yet. Means 'large'. The works!"

"Sounds delicious."

He grinned, and she watched him walk over to a man on the dock who was dressed in blue overalls, cap on his head. From his stance, hands on hips, the man looked as if he might be the foreman – or whatever they called the guy in charge over here.

She saw Harry gesture to where, only now, their car – that beautiful and so-sleek example of English hardware – was starting to rise out of the ship's hold, swinging perilously on ropes and chains.

A SHOT IN THE DARK

The man in the cap nodded. No smiles there. But she guessed Harry was doing something she had seen him do so often. A few words here and there, and suddenly people *wanted* to help him.

Doubtful he introduced himself as 'Sir', though Kat wondered whether, with the dock workers, any of that 'Lord and Lady' stuff would carry much weight.

Harry walked back.

"All tickety-boo. Er, I mean, sorted. Just explained to him what was hiding under those tarps. Asked if they had ever handled a car like that."

"And?"

"Seems he rather prefers a Bentley. Rolls Royce at a push. Though he did say if I was offering him a drive, he'd happily take it for a spin."

"Funny guy, hmm?"

"Salt of the earth."

"Well, me – I'd just slip him some money."

"Oh, see, there you go! That would *never* work here. An upstanding professional like that? He'd take it as a proper insult."

Kat doubted that. Ten years posted to American embassies from Istanbul to Tokyo had taught her one thing – a handful of dollars never failed to make the world run more smoothly.

She turned to see the Alvis roadster steadily being lowered. Slowly, she was glad to note. And – now – nothing to be alarmed about.

She turned back to Harry, watching their steamer trunks being off-loaded, to be transported to Mydworth by truck.

Lorry – not truck, she thought.

And then they would drive to their new home. "New", at least for Kat, but not to Harry. Mydworth: the small town where he grew up; a world he knew – but had been away from for so long.

Suddenly Harry wasn't checking the unloading.

"Hmm," he grunted.

"What?" she said, as he turned to look over to where the cars and taxis pulled up to pick up passengers.

Sitting there, a sleek sedan. Not a cab, but a very serious looking vehicle. And stepping out of it, now looking this way, a man crisply dressed in what looked like a chauffeur's uniform.

"Something wrong?" she said to Harry.

"Don't *know*. But I think we're about to find out."

The driver held a white envelope in his hands. He walked over directly – even urgently – to where she and Harry stood.

HARRY ALWAYS PRIDED himself on having extremely good instincts. They'd served him well back in '18 in the skies over Belgium. Also, in his various postings abroad for the Foreign Office. A few times they'd helped him avoid getting hurt.

Once even *killed*.

His every instinct told him that the envelope the man carried was unlikely to be good news.

"Sir Harry Mortimer?"

Less a question than a confirmation.

Harry gave a quick nod back. He felt Kat looking at this scene as well.

He guessed she had to be thinking: *Well, what is this about?*

The chauffeur presented the envelope to Harry. "Urgent from Whitehall, sir. I'm to wait."

Harry took the envelope, giving Kat a half grin.

"Wait? For *what*?"

He opened the tucked but unsealed envelope and removed a single piece of paper.

A SHOT IN THE DARK

He recognised the crest on the paper, the address.

The message pithily brief, but also direct.

"Harry... what is it?"

A bit of alarm in her voice there, he noted. As they had grown closer to docking at Newhaven, Harry had reassured her about their new life in his homeland.

"No more running around for me," he'd said. *"Nice quiet office job in town, driving a desk a couple of days a week, lunch at the club, home by five, no harum-scarum, hmm?"*

To which she had said: *"Doubt that."*

He took a deep breath, even as he started to wonder if there was any getting around what this letter wanted him to do.

No solution appeared as he turned to face Kat directly.

KAT COULD SEE from Harry's eyes that he wasn't happy. Took only seconds to read the words in the letter, but – whatever the message – her husband... not pleased.

"Urgent meeting. Bit of a flap on, and it seems they want me to attend."

"Really? When?" she asked. Though – with the chauffeur and limo standing by – she could figure out the answer to that one.

"Right now, apparently," he waved the offending letter. "Uses the word 'crisis' here. Chaps in the office usually show some restraint when referring to such things, so..."

"Now?"

She glanced back just as their Alvis touched down on the dock. Two men began removing the heavy tarps that had been used to protect it during its journey. A hint of the car's racing green colour caught the sunlight.

"We're *supposed* to drive to our new house together, yes? Trucks bringing everything else right behind us."

"I am still technically, um – you know – a servant of His Majesty's Government."

"Yes, and due to report in a few weeks, and even then, not a full-time position."

Harry's eyes shifted right. His beleaguered look made Kat almost withdraw her protest.

Almost.

"Tell this charming man here that you and I have things to do. You can see them tomorrow."

And then Harry did something that always cut through the slightest disagreement they had.

He took a step towards her. Bit of a smile back, not full on, but so warm – just like the night they met at that New Year's Eve reception in the British Embassy in Cairo.

He put a hand on her shoulder.

And for that moment, there was just the two of them on that dock alone.

"I *know*. But if it was you? Back in New York? Some chap from the State Department?" He paused, hand still on her shoulder – and Kat knew how this had to play out. "What would you do? What *could* you do?"

And so slowly – only now rewarding him with a smile of her own – she patted his hand on her shoulder.

"Harry. It's okay. I understand. Duty calls."

"Exactly. King and country. Ours not to reason why. And don't worry, we'll take this fellow's car into town, and I'll get Alfie to drive us back here as soon as the meeting is done with."

Alfie – someone else from Harry's life she hadn't met yet. His – what did they call them? – "batman" during the war.

A SHOT IN THE DARK

Someone who, Harry said, was fiercely loyal, and would do absolutely anything for him, even arranging things for what was going to be their London *pied-à-terre*.

"Few hours at the most, then straight back here. Pick up *our* car, and off we go, crisis over with a bit of luck."

That was the plan offered by Harry. But Kat knew it never was her style to sit around waiting, killing time.

Not when there were things to be done.

"No," she said, warm smile still on her face. "I have another idea."

Harry's turn to look surprised.

"You do?"

And Kat nodded.

2.

THE SUSSEX DOWNS

HARRY KNEW KAT well enough to know that she *definitely* could have ideas.

Nothing shy about her there.

"You get in that car there, go to London, have the meeting," she said. "Solve the crisis."

He laughed at that. "We tend to take our time solving crises around here."

He looked across – driver waiting. The lorry, loaded with their trunks, started to pull away.

"And," she said slowly, "I'll drive to our new home."

I should have seen that coming, thought Harry. The Alvis...

"Ah, right. Yes, but you see, Kat—"

He felt her bluer-than-blue eyes locked on him.

"The roads here, deuced tricky," he said. "Narrow as hell. And every now and then we have these fiendish tunnels – railway bridges, you see? Only one lane, cars coming right at each other. Take your life in your hands—"

Kat put a hand on his arm. With that touch he felt as if he had already lost the argument.

"*Harry*. I've driven the back streets of Cairo, Istanbul, Rome. I think I can deal with whatever you have here. Road atlas in the glove compartment, right?"

He nodded. Still, he thought, worth one last attempt.

"We also drive on the left. Have you ever driven on the *left?*"

"Left, right – same thing. I'll get to the house. Make sure our things are properly unloaded and put away, maybe meet this housekeeper you keep telling me about."

"Dear Maggie. You *will* like her."

"I'm sure. So… it's decided."

For a moment, he stood there. Harry had on occasion seen the odd stray American dealing with roads here. *Terrifying sight.*

"B-but then out in the country, there's the hedges, and, well, a protocol for letting cars pass, and—"

"Protocol? I know all about protocols. "

Then she took a step closer to him, her voice low. A voice that again reminded him of when he first met her.

Fell for her.

"I'll be fine."

Harry nodded, the issue settled. "All right then, well, I'd better get going. Be safe. I'll get the first train to Mydworth that I can. Pick up a cab at the station. Hopefully home not *too* long after the cocktail hour."

"You'd better be. First night, new home. Been looking forward to this."

"Me too. Well—"

He fired a look at the Alvis. Then back to Kat.

A kiss – not caring who on the dock looked.

"All right. Gotta dash."

And at that, he turned and hurried to the official car – door open, ready to go.

As he took a seat in the back, he could see Kat standing there, a smile on her face.

Then, with a last wave to her, the car pulled away from the dock, off to London.

SOMEWHERE BETWEEN Newhaven and Mydworth, Kat pulled off to the side of the road for a breather – acutely aware that she'd taken Harry's warnings much too lightly.

At first, as usual, it had been thrilling to be at the controls of the big car, the roads wide enough, the sun high, the sky blue, the sea sparkling as she drove west along the coast road towards Brighton.

Hardly any traffic, apart from sensible sedans chugging along, local delivery trucks, buses, horses and carts.

All of which she passed with graceful ease and a quick toot on the horn.

Then Brighton – the promenade road passing lines of elegant hotels and villas – and heads turning at the throaty roar of the Alvis's sporty engine.

She loved that. *This car makes an impression.*

This was England. The England she'd read about as a child and seen in so many movies. And she, Kat Reilly – daughter of a Bronx bar owner no less – was now driving through its famous towns in a shiny green sports car like a movie star, sunglasses on, hair flying in the warm air.

Kat Reilly, she thought.

Now there's a question. Am I still Kat Reilly? Or will I answer to the name – Lady Mortimer?

In this day and age? Hmm.

That was a discussion for later. Maybe after cocktails.

A SHOT IN THE DARK

But then − barrelling through one stone tunnel a little faster than was appropriate − she'd nearly sent the front end of the roadster crashing into the grille of an oncoming local bus, the driver firing an angry glance as tyres screeched and he barely slid past, the precious Alvis inches away from the stone wall.

Heart pounding from the near-miss, Kat had stuck tight to the left side of the road as the bus rumbled on, spewing smoke from the rear, passengers gawking out of the back windows at the unfamiliar sight of a speeding sports car.

And perhaps the even more unfamiliar sight of a woman driving it?

Well, she thought, staring out across fields of wheat in the late afternoon sun. *That's one lesson learned.*

Railway bridges in England *can* be tricky.

Then she released the handbrake, hit the gas, spun the wheel and gunned the Alvis back onto the road, a glimpse of dust clouds from the back wheels in the mirror.

HARRY STARED AT the Houses of Parliament, as the car glided across Westminster Bridge.

Big Ben was just striking five o'clock. As Kat would say, *"helluva time to have a meeting."* Already the pavements thronged with office workers, clerks, businessmen, all heading home, the weekend ahead.

He'd not been back in London for a couple of years − the posting in Cairo, a constant series of six-month extensions.

And now, watching the open-top buses jostling for space with cabs, cars, lorries, motorbikes, horses and carts as they all negotiated Parliament Square, he felt that old familiar thrill at being part of the hustle and bustle again.

There were a lot of great cities in the world, but none (so far!) as exciting as London. Newspaper boys calling out the evening edition of *The Post*. An old soldier, with a cap on the pavement, playing gypsy violin. A messenger boy leaping onto the rear platform of a bus as it flew by. A gaggle of laughing girls buying ice-cream from a street barrow.

How he loved this city!

He couldn't wait to share it with his new wife – the frantic fun of the place – the bars, clubs, restaurants, theatres, tea rooms, Royal Opera House, dances...

Kat – he knew – would love it as well.

And just as soon as he and Kat were settled in Mydworth, he'd bring her up here, spend a whole week in his little *pied-à-terre* in Bloomsbury, hit some parties, take advantage of his new life of semi-leisure.

Between London and Mydworth, he and Kat would have the best of both worlds. Perfect!

"Sir," said the driver – and Harry realised they'd arrived in King William Street, at the main entrance of the Foreign Office, the pavement filled with a steady stream of office workers heading home.

Harry quickly climbed out. With a nod to the driver he watched the car draw away while he adjusted his jacket and tie.

Hardly the sober affair he'd usually wear to the office – but, dammit, they'd just have to put up with it.

He turned and stared up at the enormous building that stretched all the way from Parliament Street to Horse Guards Parade.

Forget Parliament... Downing Street... this was the *real* hub of the British Empire.

A SHOT IN THE DARK

And now, in theory, his place of employment for the next few years.

He climbed the steps, against the flow of departing workers, grinned at the familiar policeman who stood, arms behind his back, guarding the entrance.

"Evening to you, Arthur!"

"Sir Harry! So good to see you back."

"Wonderful to be back." Harry looked up at the building. "I've certainly missed this place. And how's Marjory and the offspring?"

"Mustn't grumble, sir." A grin. "Not too much, at least! Little 'uns keep me young."

"Oh, I'm sure they do," said Harry smiling back.

And through the revolving doors he went, into the grand main entrance.

With luck, he thought, *I'll be out of here by six-thirty, catch the seven o'clock from Victoria, Mydworth by eight, then gin and tonics with Kat in the Dower House garden.*

KAT HAD TO admit it. She was completely lost.

The road she'd been on had climbed in sweeping curves higher and higher through dark wooded hills, until finally the gaps in the trees had opened to reveal a dizzying plateau of high, rich, farmland, with the sea maybe thirty miles away − a distant band of silver.

But somehow it was wrong. She was way off target.

She pulled over, turned the engine off and sat in the warm silence, suddenly forgetting the drive ahead, trying to let the tranquillity and peace of the English countryside wash over her. *Just for a few minutes,* she thought.

Her eyes began to close.

Whoa – Kat – wake up!

She shook her head clear and got out of the car. Then she picked up the map from the front seat and opened it fully on the low front hood of the car, trying to decode the way forward.

Surely, she couldn't be more than ten miles away from Mydworth? But the roads on the map looked more like the twisty weave of a badly knitted sweater starting to unravel.

Then she heard a *rumble*. Some kind of machine.

She looked up from the map, late afternoon sun ahead. For a country that she always heard was cloudy and gloomy all the time, the sky a deep blue. Quite beautiful.

The machine making the "rumble" came into view, emerging from a field of tall wheat just yards away.

An old tractor. Red, rusty paint peeling all over, and pulling a wooden cart behind it with a sheepdog peering over the side. The tractor steadily belched puffy grey smoke into the sky and as it got closer, the driver nodded.

Kat smiled at the man in his cap, a few days growth of beard, quizzical expression on his face.

She raised a hand.

"Excuse me. But, um, I'm wondering—" She gestured at the map. She was struggling to be heard over the rumbling engine. She said it louder. "Could you maybe, um, *show me*—" Again – to the map – even louder. "Trying to get to Mydworth!"

The man, perched so many feet higher than her, slowed the already crawling tractor until it stopped. Then, with a wheezing cough from the engine, he shut it off.

"American, hmm?" he said. "Wot you doin' here?"

"Um. Yeah. American, and what I'm doing is trying to get to Mydworth."

A SHOT IN THE DARK

"Mydworth?" he said, as if he'd never heard of the place. "*Mydworth?*"

Just my luck, thought Kat. *Meet some guy who's never left the farm.* She waited, while he scrutinised her.

"I mean, is it far?" she asked. "If you could just point—"

"Far? No, it's not *far.*" The man snorted, looked back at his dog as if checking that the sheepdog was paying attention to the conversation. "But yer goin' the wrong way, that's for sure."

Not exactly the most helpful local she ever ran into, Kat thought.

But then he climbed down from the tractor, nodded to her to follow him and crossed the road to the other side. Kat looked at the dog, who had decided to go to sleep, and followed the farmer.

He stopped at the edge of the road, then pointed across the field of wheat into a valley that lay just half a mile away.

"See that there?" he said. "That's Mydworth."

Kat followed his arm and looked down into the valley. There, nestled in a fold of hills, what looked the quintessential English town.

Something out of a picture book.

"You could walk it in five minutes," he said, "if you didn't have a car to get in the way, like."

She took in the town: a sprawl of houses and roads. A couple of church steeples. Then what looked like some grand houses in the meadows beyond. A river curving lazily down the valley.

A station, maybe half a mile from the centre – and even now, a train pulling away, steam and smoke puffing as it headed for the hills.

So that's Mydworth, she thought.

My new home.

And suddenly she didn't mind at all that she had gotten lost.

3.

WELCOME TO MYDWORTH

HARRY LOOKED DOWN the long meeting table, the air thick with cigarette smoke. Twenty or so Foreign Office experts of all kinds. Faces stern. The mood sombre.

The average age at least fifty, he thought. *Makes me the youngest in the room.*

At the other end, one of the Far East trade experts was reading aloud from an analysis of rubber exports and British investment trends over the last decade.

Really? he thought. *This is urgent?*

Was this what his working day was going to be like from now on? Interminable, boring policy meetings in smoky, windowless rooms?

Damn well hope not! Chuck the whole thing in, if it is.

He sneaked a look at his Rolex Oyster. Nearly six o'clock. This "crisis" meeting had been going an hour – and so far, he still hadn't a clue why he'd been invited.

It seemed there were rumours of a Communist uprising in Malaya. If true, British investment in the area would quickly collapse – and, overnight, fortunes could be lost.

Apparently, the Stock Exchange had already dropped on rumours of the emergency.

But Harry was a Middle East expert. The only thing he knew about rubber was that his beloved Alvis ran on Michelins.

What's all this got to do with me? he thought.

He glanced across at Sir Carlton Sinclair, chair of the meeting – and Harry's boss. He saw Carlton acknowledge the querying look, then cough loudly.

"Forgive me, gentlemen," he said. "I'm afraid that Mortimer and I have another briefing in ten minutes and we shall have to take leave of you shortly."

Harry caught the slightest flicker in Carlton's eyes.

Another briefing? Carlton hadn't mentioned it.

But Harry had the sudden thought that the real reason for his being summoned to London was perhaps soon to be revealed.

"Sir Harry is recently returned from Cairo, where – amongst other duties – he was tasked with, ahem, *monitoring* nationalist and communist organisations. I invited him along, in the hope that we might all benefit from his experience albeit in a different theatre. Sir Harry, I believe you've prepared a brief comparative analysis…"

Oh no I haven't, thought Harry, *and well you know it.*

"Perhaps you could enlighten us briefly before we hasten to our next meeting?"

Harry smiled broadly. That smile – he hoped – buying him a few seconds to prepare his non-existent analysis.

"Of course, Sir Carlton – and thank you so much for your introduction."

He opened his notebook to a page filled with dense notes (a comparison of trout streams near Mydworth that he intended to show Kat in the autumn) and ran his finger down it briefly as if to remind himself of salient points.

"Gentlemen, I'd like to start with a little background, if I may. I arrived in Cairo back in '25, as a diplomatic attaché…"

KAT DROVE SLOWLY into Mydworth, the low rumble of the Alvis bouncing off the houses in the narrow lanes.

The sidewalks (*must start calling them pavements*) were nearly empty, the stores all shut with blinds down and canopies up.

She guessed most people were already home, having their evening meal.

Their dinner? Supper? What did they call it over here?

A few cars and the odd horse and cart trundled past.

She came to a small crossroads. To the left, she saw that a cobbled road ran down towards a distant riverbank.

Ahead, the lane she was on dog-legged past a pub and then disappeared.

The pub – The King's Arms. Doors wide open, a little group of workmen sipping pints of ale, enjoying a pipe, now watching her, curious at the sight of this strange woman in a green sports car.

Must check that place out with Harry, she thought. *Right now a pint of whatever beer those guys are drinking would hit the spot.*

She looked right: a market square from the looks of it, surrounded by more stores – tearooms, bakery, newsagent. Off in one corner a water trough for horses. A water pump.

Then, at the far end, a large building, nearly as tall as the church spires – some kind of town hall, she guessed.

She stopped for a second, the lane quiet. Outside of the pub, no-one around. She dug out and checked the hand-drawn map that

Harry had made for her a month or so back – not expecting she'd be using it to navigate alone to her own home!

Then she clunked the Alvis into gear, crossed the square and drove up another little cobbled street on a gentle rise. On either side, she saw more stores now. These were the basics of town life: butcher, baker, cobbler, blacksmith, fishmonger, dairy...

The houses: two-storey, tiny upstairs windows, some leaning crookedly, looking very medieval.

At the top of the lane, another crossroads. Straight ahead, a big church and graveyard. And, on one corner, yet another pub (of course). The Green Man – looked a little fancier, with an entrance wide enough for cars, and even a restaurant attached.

Another glance at Harry's map, and she made a left there, and then a right into a dirt track that led around behind the church, rising up a slow hill out of the town.

If she'd read the map right – this was the way to the Dower House.

And with luck, Harry's housekeeper Maggie would have the whole place ready, beds aired, maybe a fire lit, coffee brewing.

She smiled. Already the place sounding like home.

HARRY RAN FULL-OUT down Victoria Street, dodging the early evening theatre crowds that thronged the pavements.

Two minutes to catch the train! God!

Past the buses, the line of taxis, then into a packed Victoria Station, teeming with people, the air thick with smoke and steam, noisy with newspaper-sellers, porters shouting, the screech of carriage wheels and puffing engines.

His eyes locked on the big indicator boards to check the platform for Mydworth, and he set off again through the jostling crowds of commuters, dropping a shoulder to get past a burly porter, nearly having to hurdle an empty trolley.

Making good use of his rugby skills.

A look at his watch. One minute left.

Ticket in hand, Harry raced onto the platform just as the guard's whistle blew. The great Southern steam engine – already chuffing, wheels spinning, the carriages clattering and clunking – began to pull away.

Harry ran down the platform, reaching for a door, any door, pulling it open – a quick hop and a jump – somebody's hands reaching out to grab him and pull him aboard.

And then he was *in*, pulling the door shut with the leather strap and slamming the window closed to keep the smoke and steam out! *Made it*, he thought.

A look around the carriage, and – squeezing into a spot – he sank back into the musty upholstery, nodding to the other occupants and the elderly gentleman next to him who shuffled along the crowded bench seat to give him space.

"Thanks, old chap!" he said, turning and looking across at the bowler-hatted commuter who'd pulled him in.

"Cutting it fine there," said the man, taking out *The Times* and folding it carefully.

Stating the obvious.

Must remember the peccadilloes of my countrymen. Been a while, thought Harry

"Wife'll absolutely kill me if I'm not home for dinner," he said.

A phrase he'd heard so many times on this route as a single man – but never imagined he'd ever utter.

I'm married, he thought. *Isn't* that *interesting. And to a yank no less!*

"Oh, dear me, yes," said the old fellow next to Harry. "It's surprising how few such murders come to trial."

A SHOT IN THE DARK

The man obviously liked to read his paper and offer a running commentary.

The other passengers laughed politely, and Harry turned to smile at them – but their heads were already deep in their evening papers again.

He turned to the window, ready to watch the familiar path of his homecoming.

The train rattled over the Thames now, past Chelsea Bridge. To one side, he could see Battersea Park, families relaxing, enjoying the early evening sun. To his left, an enormous building site – the foundations, he guessed, for London's great new power station.

And as he took in all this – the old and the new – he pondered on Sir Carlton's words in that brief meeting in his private office.

It seemed the Foreign Office had in mind a *lot* of ways to use Harry on his two or three days a week.

"No stodgy meetings, Harry. Chap like you – your talent, your abilities – we intend to use all of that."

Then the most intriguing part…

"Can't say exactly what may be on offer. But I can promise you this. You won't be bored."

Sir Carlton's words were – well – rather amazing.

What exactly would be on "offer"? What kind of work? Undoubtedly secret. That was clear. Important, too.

And perhaps – Harry guessed – even dangerous?

KAT STOOD AND stared at the Dower House.

Okay, she thought, *the place itself looks – well – very English.*

Thick climbing plants – with broad leaves and purple flowers – worked their way up two small pillars at the entrance, and then filled the walls below three second-floor windows.

Down on the ground floor, one tall window on each side of the solid front door.

Only one problem.

The shutters were all... shut. The house was empty and locked. And a note on the front door said: *"Trunks returned to depot, redeliver Monday 8am."*

So, that meant that the truck had got here before her, found nobody home and disappeared for the weekend.

Nice.

And what about Maggie what's-her-name – Harry's "incredibly amazing" housekeeper?

Wasn't she supposed to be ready with a homecoming meal after the journey all the way from Cairo? Ten days by boat and car and not even a cup of coffee for a welcome?

Kat shrugged.

No use getting worked up about it. Things happen.

Perhaps there had been some kind of mix-up. Maybe Harry's telegram from Marseilles, the one with the change of travel plans, never reached the housekeeper?

Kat stepped back and checked her watch. Seven thirty. What time did it get dark round here? She looked up at the sky – sun nearly set. *Soon.*

She shrugged, her old field training kicking in. *List options. Evaluate. Act.*

So, what were the options? One. Wait here for Harry. *Hmm – cold – and could be a long wait.*

Two. Go stay in a hotel in town. *Maybe – if she'd seen one. But she hadn't. Place must have one, though?*

Three. Pub? Get a few drinks with the locals and wait for Harry. *Tempting – but probably not the homecoming Harry was expecting.*

Four. Go find Harry's aunt, her house, and – well – meet the family. She waited a moment.

Well, *hell yes*. Option four. Wasn't that the obvious one? What were families for? And didn't Harry's Aunt Lavinia – *Lady Lavinia*, she reminded herself – have a grand place right up the road?

She pulled out the crumpled sketch map she'd used to find the Dower House, straightened it out and peered at it.

Sure enough, there was a path leading from the back of the house across a couple of fields right up to the front door of what Harry labelled "the Mortimer country seat".

Mydworth Manor.

Now – didn't that sound like the kind of establishment where a girl could get a stiff drink and a meal when she needed one?

And she definitely needed both.

She grabbed her jacket from the back seat of the Alvis, and clipped the tonneau in place, giving the car a roof in case it rained. *After all, didn't it always rain in England?*

Then she scribbled a note for Harry and pinned it to the front door.

With luck, he'd be home in an hour and they could all have a little family get-together with Aunt Lavinia, while Harry dug out some keys to the house so they could come back here and get some sleep.

She headed through the garden – stopping to sniff a *totally lush* rosebush on the way – then slipped through a cute little picket gate and headed off across a broad meadow.

After five minutes, she paused. Pulled out the sketch again and inspected it carefully.

She'd expected the manor house to come into view by now, but all she could see was the far range of wooded hills.

No matter – the meadow sloped gently upwards – the Mortimer estate was probably just in the valley beyond.

Aunt Lavinia is going to be so *surprised to see me*, she thought, in the gathering dusk.

Though, well she knew, sometimes surprises aren't always welcome.

4.

A DEATH AT THE MANOR

HARRY SLAMMED the compartment door shut and watched the train slowly chug away from Mydworth station, heading into the darkness and to the coast.

Then he followed the other commuters past the ticket hall and round into the tiny station yard where taxis sometimes waited.

But the yard was empty. He checked his watch in the light of the single street lamp.

Not worth waiting – best a brisk walk up through the town to the house.

Should only take twenty minutes, he thought, and he set off up the hill.

KAT CLAMBERED over a fence, slipped – and landed with a thud, on her face, on the wet grass.

"Damn," she said out loud. "Damn, damn, damn."

Then she stood up, wiped the mud off her khaki trousers and top – selected for how she thought they made her look like one of her idols, the amazing Amelia Earhart.

Now, the whole outfit was stained with muddy circles.
Oh well.

Half an hour she'd been walking – *so much for Harry's renowned map-making skills*. So far, she'd crossed one stream, avoided a herd of cows, and lost a shoe in a hedge. Now covered in mud, her remaining shoe... useless.

Not quite the evening she'd been expecting.

But hey – it can only get better, she thought. She carried on across the meadow, avoiding what they called *cowpies* at home.

Luckily a half-moon had risen, and there was just enough light to chart a course.

And then in the distance she heard music – familiar music.

Fats Waller!

The voice carrying clearly over the meadow...

"Ain't Misbehavin'. Saving all my love for you."

Extraordinary! Fats himself, right here in the English countryside!

She headed towards the sound, and minutes later reached the crest of the hill to see – down in the valley, only a couple of hundred yards away – a large country house.

It made the Dower House look like a hut.

"Wow, wow, wow," she said – this time in a hushed voice – as she stopped and took in the unexpected sight and sounds.

Looking stocky and square, the house squatted behind perfect lawns dotted with classical statues, surrounded by woodland.

She could also see easily a dozen bedroom windows, framed by thick ivy across the upper floors; a grand entrance with glowing lanterns; and a sweeping gravel drive that came out of the woods and curved round a fountain, with a cherub armed with bow and arrow, set back from the house.

And even from up here, the source of the music was clear: a large downstairs living room, or whatever they called it here,

A SHOT IN THE DARK

running along the side of the building, with French windows thrown wide open, and a dozen or so people standing inside, all in evening dress, chatting, laughing.

Drinking cocktails!

A pause in the music – and then the gramophone launched into a new disc – a song that she and Harry absolutely loved back in Cairo: *Let's Do It, Let's Fall in Love.*

Which of course is exactly what we did, she thought.

Albeit, less a decision than, in her opinion – inevitable.

Hell, yes! This is more like it, she thought, a thrill of excitement making up for the crazy hike through muddy fields. *First night in England, and we're going to a party, Kat!*

She brushed a stray piece of straw from her hair and wiped her muddy hands on her jacket.

Guess I'll have to borrow some clothes. And definitely some shoes.

With a skip in her step, she headed barefoot down the gentle slope towards the house.

KAT WALKED ACROSS the dark shadowed lawn of Mydworth Manor watching the smartly-dressed guests being gently ushered out of the reception room and into a formal dining room: tall windows revealed a long table set with candelabra, glass and silver sparkling, maids and footmen ready to serve dinner.

Well – isn't this something, she thought.

She suddenly realised that in this muddy state – she might *not* quite get the welcome she was hoping for.

Maybe better to head for the servants' entrance and enlist some help getting an outfit?

Don't want to frighten Aunt Lavinia – or the elegant guests!

She walked a bit closer to the house, trying to figure the layout. To one side stood what she guessed were outbuildings and stables – in the darkness, she could just see the outline of cars parked in a line.

As she rounded the side of the house, searching for a servants' entrance, she glanced up at the bedroom windows.

In one of them, she saw something – a shape and shadows moving.

Must be somebody late for dinner, she thought. *Better hurry up – smells good – don't want to miss it!*

But then, before she looked away, a man appeared at the window, silhouetted against the bedroom light. She watched him grab hold of the window frame – then climb up onto it!

And now, through the open window, she heard loud voices coming from the room.

What the…?

She saw the man pivot, as if to climb out of the window, his foot reaching down into the ivy and trellis for a footing, his body now fully twisted round so his back was to her, one hand gripping the window frame, one reaching down to get a hold in the ivy.

A shrill scream from inside the room.

A piercing, terrifying, woman's scream.

And, right at that window, a muzzle flash and a gunshot – crisp and loud out here in the gardens.

And the clinging man fell backwards, as if punched, falling, head rocking back, arms spiralling, legs now in the air, kicking, taking forever to land. Kat knew he must land so hard from that height.

With a horrible thud, he hit the ground.

Kat stood still, not moving, mouth open in shock, not able to say or do anything for a second. Another man appeared at the window, arm raised, revolver in hand and...

Bang!

A second gunshot, this one somehow seeming louder - as if the first shot had silenced the world. The muzzle flash brighter too -

Bang!

And now a third.

And Kat felt, rather than heard, the bullet thread through the air near her, and realised *she* was in the firing line. For the second time that day, instincts kicked in and she crouched and ran towards the nearest cover: a milky-white stone pedestal plinth, with a helmeted figure atop it holding a sword in one hand, and a head in another.

And as she reached it, stumbling, falling – she hit somebody hard with her shoulder who fell back with the impact against the pedestal with a loud...

"What the bloody hell—?"

"Harry?" she said, grabbing a familiar-feeling arm, as yet another two shots rang out.

Bang! Bang!

And a fragment of marble shattered above their heads.

"Kat? Can I not leave you for an afternoon without a war starting?"

"I didn't start *this* one."

"Good to hear. Um, any idea what's going on?"

"None at all. But there's a man down, over in the bushes there. Fell from the window."

"Uninvited guest perhaps? Got your note by the way."

"Yes, gathered that."

Bang! Kat saw a chunk of muddy grass spiral away into the darkness by her feet. She tucked in her legs a little more.

"Okay, so I'm a bit late to this party," said Harry. "Out of interest – how many shots *is* that?"

Kat thought for a second.

"Six – I think."

"*Think?*"

"No – I'm sure."

"Good," said Harry. "Sounds like a standard-issue Webley. He'll have to stop to reload."

Kat watched her husband stand and brush down his suit, then shout up to the window: "I say! Do you mind awfully cutting that out, somebody could get hurt."

Bang!

"Ah," said Kat, confused. "Sorry. *That* must be six. Though, Harry – I *really* do think it was seven."

"Counting. Always tricky at times like this."

She stood up too, grabbed her surviving shoe, and looked across at the house. More lights were now on, and people were crowding at the downstairs windows. She heard shouting and crying from up in the bedrooms.

"Harry. The man who fell…" she said, knowing that seconds could mean the difference between life and death. "Come on."

With Harry just behind her, she ran towards the house.

There, in the shrubs and flowers below the window from where the shots had been fired, she could see a dark shape.

The body of a man, lying on his back, not moving. Limbs splayed. The angles – unnatural.

She crouched down next to him, her fingers quickly reaching to the neck, looking for a pulse. His skin was still warm, the eyes blankly open. A young man. A lock of dark hair falling across his forehead.

Harry was at her side. "Anything?"

She hated it when there was nothing she could do.

"No," she said. "He's dead."

5.

THE CONSTABLE CALLS

KAT STEPPED BACK, as Harry crouched and leaned in to inspect the body.

"Quite a drop," he said, nodding towards the bedroom window. But then he tilted the man's head gently, and the lock of hair fell away: "But – I don't think it was the fall that killed him."

In the darkness, Kat could now make out a bullet wound to the man's temple, blood glistening.

As a young volunteer nurse in France, back in 1918, she'd seen enough casualties to know that such a wound was almost certainly fatal.

She felt Harry's hand – warm on her arm, felt his body next to hers, knowing that he understood what she was feeling now.

Both of them had that shared history of war. In moments like this it could return without warning, raw and vivid.

She stood up – Harry's arm still on her shoulder – then turned as a woman's voice cut loudly through the silence.

"Good *God!* Harry? Is that *you?*"

From out of the darkness, a flashlight was suddenly pointed at her and Harry, as a group of figures rushed towards them. "Hell-lo Aunt Lavinia," said Harry, shielding his eyes from the dazzle.

As the flashlight was lowered and the group approached, Kat saw a tall, elegant woman leading them, the brightly coloured Japanese silk shawl over her shoulders catching the moonlight perfectly.

So... this is the famous Lavinia, thought Kat, taking in her every feature.

Harry had told her so much about his aunt – but not how striking she was.

Tall, like Harry, with a kind of languor about her movements.

Her hair was dark and fashionably short – with the type of kiss curls you'd normally see on a younger woman. Her clothes elegant, her face sharply defined, with high cheek bones and barely any make-up.

She looks like... like a... leopard, thought Kat.

Lavinia stopped suddenly – clearly shocked to see Harry – and then even more shocked to see the body at their feet.

"Oh my," said Lavinia, focusing the torchlight on the body, then taking Harry's hand as if to steady herself. "Poor boy. Is he... *dead?*"

"Afraid so," said Harry. "You know him?"

Kat watched Lavinia lean closer, then pull back quickly.

"Oh God – it's Coates. My driver."

"I'm sorry," said Harry. "Any idea what happened?"

"Heard a gunshot. From the look of things, I think Cousin Reggie shot him," said Lavinia, looking up at the still-lit bedroom window above. "As to why? I have absolutely no idea."

"I think perhaps I do," said Harry. Kat watched as he took out a handkerchief, crouched down by the body, reached into the man's jacket pocket... and gently pulled out an ornate diamond necklace.

As he stood – the jewellery sparkled and shimmered in the light from the house. Kat heard a gasp from the small crowd of onlookers behind her.

"Extraordinary," said Lavinia.

"That's not all," said Harry, nodding towards the flowerbed. And now, Kat could see the light catching other pieces, scattered on the ground: single jewels, bracelets, rings...

The man must have held them clutched in his hand as he fell.

Kat watched Harry fold the handkerchief with the necklace and place it in his trouser pocket. Then he took off his jacket and gently placed it over the body.

After a few seconds, he rose and faced the small group of onlookers, in their evening dress, who now pressed closer.

"There's nothing we can do for him now," he said, gently ushering Lavinia's guests away from the crime scene. "I suggest we all move back to the house and telephone for the police."

Kat watched Lavinia and the group turn and walk towards the brightly lit portico of the great house. Then Harry put his arm back around her shoulder and they followed.

"Harry. I really *did* hear six shots," said Kat, quietly.

"Oh, I believe you did," said Harry. "Numbers are a strong suit with you."

"Odd, don't you think?"

"Very. We'll get you a hot bath and a whisky later and talk about that, eh? But in the meantime..." Harry looked at the crowd walking in. "Let's, um, keep that to ourselves for now, hmm?"

Kat nodded. Having that same instinct.

"DARLING HARRY," Lavinia said once the other guests had gone back into the house, leaving just the three of them waiting for the police on the elegant stone steps. "It's a joy to have you home again. But what on *earth* were you doing in the garden?"

"Oh dear. Did you not receive my telegram? Got rather bored in Marseilles, so we loaded up the old Alvis and set a course for England so I could..." he paused, still blinking in the light "...introduce you to my wife."

Lavinia turned and stared at Kat.

That look. Not terribly warm, Kat thought.

Was it the missing shoes? The mud?

Or amidst all the elegant gowns – her pants?

Um, trousers, she reminded herself.

In the bright electric light, Kat looked down at her ripped, muddied and tattered clothes, then swapped the one remaining shoe from her right to her left hand.

A wipe on her jacket.

"Lovely to meet you, Lady Lavinia," Kat said, hoping she'd remembered the correct way to address Harry's aunt, and holding out her hand. She saw Lavinia inspect it, as if she'd offered her some kind of wet fish, before finally taking it.

"The pleasure's all mine, I'm sure," said Lavinia, though Kat suspected the welcome was being delivered through clenched teeth.

The awkward moment was saved by the sound of a jangling bell approaching.

Back in the Bronx that sound would have meant the ice-cream guy was coming. But Kat knew from her time in Cairo that British police cars played bells, not sirens.

She stood next to Harry and watched the car's lights approaching through the trees, shadows flickering across the dark lawn.

"Not quite the homecoming I'd imagined," he said softly, as Lavinia stepped to one side to talk to a butler, who had emerged from the house.

"Me neither," said Kat.

"Love the outfit, by the way," he whispered. "You should wear straw more often."

HARRY WATCHED HIS aunt calmly issue orders to Benton the butler, then hurry back to his side.

"Harry – would you mind helping me deal with this? Police and all that?"

From the look, Harry wasn't sure the invite extended to his just-introduced bride. But he said, keeping his voice low, "Of course, Aunt Lavinia. Best your guests stay inside while *we* tend to things, yes?"

He looked at Kat, meaning: *This means you too, kid.*

Lavinia nodded. "I do believe – despite the unfortunate event – the extended cocktail hour will keep them engaged. And there's no shortage of things to chatter about now, that's for sure."

With a final look at her guests, all muttering to each other as Benton led them back to the reception room with a fresh tray of drinks, Lady Lavinia stepped forward as the police car pulled up, with a slide of gravel, at the entrance to Mydworth Manor.

KAT WATCHED THE two officers step out of the car and approach Harry's aunt, their faces appropriately grim.

One on the tall side, portly with a well-tended moustache. The other, shorter and significantly thinner, and sporting a miniature replica of the same moustache.

"M'lady," the portly one said, "we came soon as possible."

"Yes, very brisk, Sergeant." Lavinia turned to look back to where Kat and Harry stood, just a step behind. "This is my nephew, Sir Harry Mortimer, and his wife, um, Lady Mortimer."

She had trouble getting that one out, Kat noted.

The sergeant stared at Kat, clearly thrown by her appearance.

Probably thinks I'm the gardener, thought Kat.

Then he recovered and tipped his hat, politely. "Sergeant Timms, sir, and" – the slightest nod to the other officer – "Constable Thomas." For a moment, it seemed all were unsure exactly what to do next. "Now then, perhaps we'd better examine the victim?"

With a quick look to Harry, Lavinia tossed the ball to him.

"Er, yes," he said. "This way. Not a pretty sight, I'm afraid."

And Kat followed her husband as he led the local police to where the corpse lay.

KAT STOOD BACK and watched, as Harry removed his jacket from the body, and both the sergeant and his constable aimed their torches down, moving from bloodied head to foot and back again.

So strange, she thought, *to be standing here next to a dead body.*

Again, no-one said anything.

"And he *is*, m'lady?"

"Alfred Coates. My driver."

Kat watched the constable lean down, looking genuinely curious.

As perhaps this might be the first body he'd ever seen.

"Shot in the head, m'lady," the constable said, back to standing erect, announcing the discovery as if he had found a great prize.

"Apparently," said Lavinia.

Sergeant Timms cleared his throat, took out a notebook and pen, and started to make notes.

"So. Alfred Coates? With an 'e' I assume?"

Kat saw Lavinia nod. The policeman was clearly trying her patience.

"Thank you," said Timms.

Then he continued. "From the" – he gestured at the body – "looks of things, hard to tell if it was the shot that killed him or the fall which ensued."

Kat was tempted to point out that a bullet to the head is usually fatal. But she held her tongue.

"Either way," Lavinia said, waving at the air above the grim scene, "he *is* dead, poor fellow. And, well, this is all rather *new* to me. What do we do?"

Kat noticed that Harry, never at a loss for words, was staying rather quiet.

It was a side of him that she knew he brought to his work. Life was usually a romp for Harry, and a great one too, until things turned serious.

And then – he was a match for anything.

"We'll call the coroner, m'lady. Roust him out of bed if need be. Have this dealt with. I'll, um, need to speak to all and sundry, of course. Your guests. Find out exactly what happened."

Harry's voice came back into the conversation, low and direct.

"They're all in there," he said. "Including the man who shot him."

"Ah. So, you've apprehended the culprit already?" said Constable Thomas.

"I'd hardly call Cousin Reggie a 'culprit'," said Lavinia.

"Reggie?" said Timms.

"If I may," said Harry, "the, er, victim was shot by one of my aunt's guests, Lord Tamworth, while apparently climbing out of," Harry pointed up the second floor, "that window."

Timms nodded, jotting down more notes as Harry continued. "While carrying *these*."

At this, Kat saw Harry remove the handkerchief from his pocket and unfold it, to reveal the diamond necklace.

"They were in Coates's jacket pocket."

Timms looked at the jewels, mouth open. "Right."

"More jewellery scattered all around the body," said Harry. "From the fall."

"I see."

"I expect you'll be putting a man on guard duty, soon as, sergeant, yes?"

"Sir?" said Timms. "Ah, yes, of course. Make sure nothing gets touched during the night." He fired a look and a nod at Constable Thomas. "We'll first need to ask questions, um… take names—"

Kat thought that the sergeant sounded as if he was making up the rules of this evening as he went along.

Lavinia took a step towards the man.

"Oh, thank you, Sergeant. It's a dreadful business. Very distressing for everybody. But I totally understand, you must do what you must."

"Thank you, m'lady. I shall have to ascertain of course the full course of events. How your driver came to be… er… hanging from the upstairs window. And why it was deemed… umm… *necessary* to shoot him. Constable Thomas and I will meanwhile get on the car radio and, as I said—"

"I know. The coroner."

Lavinia stepped over to Harry and Kat, and gestured to the great stone steps that led into the manor house.

"Shall we?"

And while the two policemen hurried to the police car, still with its glaring lights on, Lady Lavinia walked with Harry and Kat back to the house.

KAT CROSSED THE threshold of Mydworth Manor for the first time and took in the amazing interior. Black and white marble floor tiles stretched for twenty or thirty feet in every direction. Above her head hung a massive chandelier, sparkling with electric lights.

And ahead, a grand double staircase with polished handrails rose to a first-floor gallery and presumably led to who-knows-how-many corridors of bedrooms beyond.

On the walls, Kat saw ancestral portraits. In some, the likeness to Harry was instantly clear – those dark, piercing eyes.

A young maid stood at the foot of the stairs.

Kat could see the girl had been crying – her eyes red and bloodshot. She watched as Lavinia went over to her, said a few quiet words, then handed over her shawl. The girl nodded, gave a weak smile, then slipped away through a door that Kat guessed led below stairs.

Years ago, back in Manhattan, Kat herself had worked on the staff of a wealthy New York family.

She could imagine the shock the sudden violent death of a fellow servant must be causing.

"Harry," said Lavinia, turning back to Harry and touching his wrist. "Stay close to Sergeant Timms, would you? See what he learns?"

"Glad to, Aunt Lavinia," said Harry, nodding. "Kat too, of course."

Kat saw Lavinia's eyes widen – as if Harry had suggested they all go peel off their clothes and dance in the fountain.

Now there's an idea, she thought.

"*Both* of you?" said Lavinia. "I mean, are you sure that's appropriate?"

"Absolutely," said Harry, grinning. "Oh and, I wonder, it seems, what with the Dower House all locked up, and trunks not coming back till Monday, we're rather short of a bed for the night—"

"Of *course*! I'll have the housekeeper provide you and—"

There, thought Kat, *she's stumped. Whatever will she call me?*

"–your... wife... with a room. And a change of clothes, perhaps?"

This, thought Kat, *is going to be a tough one.*

Lady Lavinia clearly loved Harry, and she knew that Harry felt the same.

Now the task will be for me to find a way into all that.

But then – I do like challenges.

Kat chose to answer, "Thank you, Lady Lavinia. That is so kind."

Lavinia answered, her voice dead earnest. "I would not have it any other way. And please," a look to Harry, "do call me 'Lavinia'."

And now was the time.

"I'm Kat. Short for Katherine"

"How terribly... *modern.*"

So far, talking to Lavinia was more like playing tennis.

"Ah, Sergeant Timms," she said, stepping away from them and gliding across the marble floor towards the front door, where Kat saw the policeman had reappeared.

She watched him brush his feet on the immense doormat, then take off his hat and lay it gingerly on a small table.

Probably not the usual house he entered in his line of work.

"The guests are through here, Sergeant," said Lavinia, gesturing towards a set of doors that Benton had opened wide. And then they all walked into the great reception room, the murmur of voices reaching the foyer, accompanied by the rattling of ice in glasses.

6.

THE MAN WHO FIRED THE GUN

FOR A MOMENT, Harry waited while his aunt went over to the butler to arrange things.

He could see the guests standing in a small group at the far end of the great reception room – no doubt talking about the extraordinary events of the evening.

Harry nodded a greeting to one or two who acknowledged him – though he didn't recognise any of the faces as being local.

London friends of Lavinia's, no doubt, he thought. *So much for their peaceful weekend jaunt in the country.*

Then, before joining the sergeant, he turned to Kat. "At least we have a place to sleep tonight."

She smiled.

Taking this all in good spirits, he thought.

"Though – not *quite* the cosy night in I'd imagined," Harry said.

"No. And definitely not – what's the word? – the 'staid' old England I'd imagined."

"Ah, yes. Well, you'll learn that where my aunt is involved, *staid* is never the problem."

"I don't think she likes me."

"Well, *probably* not. Yet. She *is* English, of course. Such a thing as liking people does take some time over here. Only just met you and all that, right? But I think, in time, you will have more in common with her than you'd believe."

He saw Kat gesture towards the sergeant, who pulled a small black notebook out of his back pocket.

"I think the 'investigation' is about to begin," she said. "We'll just go tag along with him, shall we?"

Harry nodded, and saw the sergeant have another word with Lady Lavinia, who now pointed at a man and a woman, sitting close together on an ornate love seat, red brocade and gold thread catching the sparkling light of the brilliant chandeliers overhead.

The sergeant nodded as he slowly walked over.

The two people, hands interlocked, sat forward, looking shell-shocked.

Harry knew who they were, although he'd only met them once, so many years ago at a family funeral.

Cousin Reggie and his wife Claudia. Lord and Lady Tamworth.

He gave a small nod to Kat, and then, casually – as if only mildly curious – the two of them walked over to the couple, who only now looked up at the barrel-chested police sergeant standing right in front of them.

SERGEANT TIMMS didn't seem to mind – Kat thought – that she and Harry had come close behind him, with Lavinia also hovering nearby as well.

"Um, Lord and Lady Tamworth, yes?" said Timms. "So terrible what has happened. But there's just a few questions I need to ask you both tonight, if you don't mind."

A SHOT IN THE DARK

Kat watched the wife – Lady Tamworth – sinewy, tall, with dark hair stylishly cropped. Her eyes, though, wide with whatever horror she had just seen.

But she looked to her husband, Lord Tamworth to reply. Not quite a visual match for her. Sitting on the loveseat, Reggie seemed on the smallish side. But his eyes also looked wide, as if he too were still reeling from the shock.

Not every day you shoot a man while he's climbing out your bedroom window.

"Of course," Reggie said. "Absolutely."

"Um, perhaps you can tell me what exactly happened here tonight?"

"Sergeant, yes, well, you see, it was just before dinner. We were all having drinks, down here. Must have been around a quarter past eight. At some point my wife told me she had to return our room briefly."

"Was nothing, really," said Claudia. "But if I hadn't gone back—"

Lord Tamworth quickly patted her hand.

"There, there." Then he looked back up at the police officer.

"I carried on chatting to people – you know? Decent crowd, Lady Lavinia's friends. Everyone having a perfectly genial evening, nothing out of the ordinary. Anyway, Benton announces dinner, and, well, I realise Claudia's not yet down, so I pop back up see if everything's all right—"

Kat saw Lord Tamworth wait, while Sergeant Timms scribbled all this down.

"Anyway, soon as I got near the room, I heard voices – rather sinister voices."

"Sinister?" said Timms.

"Nasty. Threatening. I pushed open our bedroom door – but the room was empty. The voices were coming from the dressing room next door. Door was closed, you see."

"Yes," said Timms. "I see."

"I could tell something bad was up, straight away. Claudia here – well – it sounded like she was in pain. And, as I said, a man's voice – angry. Harsh – you know?"

"Yes, sir. Think I got that."

"So – something definitely amiss, no doubt about it. So, I grabbed the old Army revolver from my case, pulled open the dressing room door…"

Kat was aware that by now the whole room had gone quiet. She could see the group of guests at the far end, glasses in hand, staring, eyes wide at this dramatic account.

"And what exactly did you see, sir?"

"Pretty dreadful sight, I can tell you! Claudia on the floor, sobbing her damn eyes out, terrible state. And two men in the room! One man still at my wife's jewellery case, the other, tall, dark-haired fellow, already at the window, escaping! Just got the barest glimpse of him."

"Robbing you, is that what you suspected?"

Timms does like the obvious questions, Kat thought.

"Well what do you bloody think, man? Of course, robbing us! Chap had a case of my wife's jewels in his hand," Lord Tamworth carried on. "So, I pointed the old Webley at the fella in the room – and shouted at him – put your hands up or I shoot, something like that, don't remember the exact words."

Kat felt Harry shift a bit, standing close.

And she thought: *My husband's about to join this party.*

"Um, Cousin Reggie. Been a while. Oh, this is my wife, Kat."

A SHOT IN THE DARK

Reggie and his wife now looked up at the two of them with even more confusion.

"Ah, yes – Harry. Right. Heard you were out East m'boy? You back then? What a night you picked!"

"Well, yes. We're *just* back, and I'm so terribly sorry this has happened to you. In Mydworth Manor, too. *Whatever* is the world coming to?"

Kat watched Reggie nod at this bit of pleasantry in the midst of telling the police how a man happened to be shot in the head only minutes earlier.

"But I was just wondering," said Harry. "Handy thing that, having a gun. You always travel that way?"

Now Kat caught Sergeant Timms look over, trusty notepad open, and – from his pursed lips – she could see he wasn't thrilled that his line of questioning had been interrupted.

"Well, yes. I mean heading up to London later in the week, and *these* days, so many desperate people there. Best to be safe than sorry, that's what I say to dear Claudia here."

Kat also caught Lord Tamworth's wife – this Claudia – nod. But the woman also looked rather directly at Harry.

A little bit too directly, Kat thought.

Timms cleared his throat.

"So – you gave the man a warning?" he said, hoping to get the story going again.

"Oh absolutely. Made it very damn clear what my intentions were. Stop or I'll shoot!"

"And what did he do?"

"Totally ignored me! Bloody fool. Just stuffed the jewels in his pocket – scrambled for the window."

"And your wife, sir?"

"Oh, I made sure Lady Tamworth was well out of the way. The first man already gone, down the damned trellis with half the jewels, the second now on the window sill, couldn't let him get away, so I fired."

"At his head?" Timms asked.

Again, asking the obvious.

"Why yes. Outside of his hands holding on for dear life, it was about the only target, I'm afraid."

"Hit him then, that first shot, m'lord?"

Reggie nodded. A small smile. "Picked up quite a reputation as a marksman during the war, don't you know."

Kat saw Harry look at her. *Something about this… interesting him.*

"And the other shots?"

Claudia opened her mouth as if about to speak, but her husband hurried on.

"I ran to the window, obviously. The man I'd shot now lay on the ground, but this other chap who'd grabbed a case too, he was down there on the lawn, racing through the garden."

"You had no doubt that this second man had your jewels as well?" Timms said.

"None at all. Know what my wife's jewellery cases look like, obviously."

"So, between them – I imagine these two fellows got away with quite a haul, sir?" said Timms.

At this point, Kat saw Claudia start to sob.

"That first man had nearly everything," said Claudia. "Everything."

Reggie put a hand on her knee, patted gently.

"Yes – all gone."

"How terribly distressing for you both," said Harry. "I wonder – just curious – do you always travel with the jewellery?"

"Good Lord no," said Reggie. "But you see – we're staying here *en route* to the State banquet for the King and Queen of Afghanistan, on Tuesday. Had to bring the sparklers. All stops out for that event. Buck Pal! Tails, tiaras, the whole caboodle."

Kat had a question as this tale unfolded. Actually, she had a few questions rumbling around in her head. But with Harry and the sergeant already at it, she bided her time.

"Indeed. And those jewels – I imagine – are very valuable" Harry asked, sounding perfectly casual.

Lady Tamworth answered this time, only two words but said with a grim solemnity.

"A *fortune*."

"Fortune," said Timms, speaking as he wrote in his notebook. "I don't suppose you could elaborate, m'lord? M'lady?"

Kat saw Reggie look at Claudia who shrugged, then put her head in her hands.

"Hmm," said Reggie. "Both cases. Tiaras. Necklaces. Ear-rings. Diamonds all of 'em!"

"Bearing in mind, sir, we will be able to recover one of the cases," said Timms.

"Ah yes, of course. The other case. At a guess – ten thousand."

"Ten thousand pounds, sir?" said Timms, nearly dropping his notebook.

"Guineas, of course."

Kat realised the whole room had gone quiet. Hardly surprising. The figure – immense. No wonder Lord Tamworth had pulled a gun on the thieves.

She looked at Harry, who gave a barely perceptible raise of the eyebrows. She wondered if he had the same thought she did.

This was no casual robbery.

This must have been planned. Somebody *knew* the jewels were going to be there.

A professional job, for sure.

A SHOT IN THE DARK

7.

QUESTIONS OVER

"WHAT ABOUT this other man – the one who got away?" asked Harry. "Did you get a good look at him?"

"Yes," Timms concurred, jumping in, "what of him?"

Kat knew what they were both thinking. A manhunt needed organising – but first, they needed a description.

"Dashed away into the darkness. Fired as best I could. But he zigged, zagged, this way, that! And nearly impossible to see."

Finally, Kat couldn't resist.

"But you did somehow fire at the statue. That I was crouched behind."

"Ah, I see. That was you was it? Terribly sorry, my dear. In the darkness, saw a bit of movement there, and thought the blaggard had maybe taken refuge behind the statue. Hope it didn't give you a fright?"

Made some sense, Kat thought, though it seemed to her that – for a marksman – those shots were going all over the place.

"Not at all, Lord Tamworth."

"*Reggie*, please," he said, smiling at her.

"And you didn't recognise the man, sir?" said Timms. "Never seen him before?"

Reggie seemed to think about that, then: "No, don't think so." Then he turned to his wife: "My dear?"

"No, never," she said, shaking her head: "Tall. Horrible man. Dark hair."

"Age?" asked Timms. "Young? Old?"

Kat saw Reggie and Claudia shrug and look to each other.

"Only got the briefest glimpse of course, but – thirties?" said Reggie. "Forties perhaps?"

Timms jotted in his notepad – looking rather exasperated, Kat observed.

That description could apply to half the men in the country.

"And this chap – this Coates – did you notice him at all while you were staying here?" said Timms.

"In what way 'notice' him, Sergeant?" asked Claudia.

"I mean, the fellow was Lady Lavinia's driver here at Mydworth. I wonder, did you ever see him in the house? Hanging about upstairs perhaps – where he shouldn't have been? Anything suspicious?"

"No," said Claudia. "He may have been the driver here, but I'd never seen him before in my life."

"Me neither," said Reggie. "And – I'll tell you one thing, Sergeant – I'm glad I never shall again."

A movement at the door – and Kat saw that the young constable had appeared. Benton motioned him across to Sergeant Timms.

The constable leaned close and whispered something to his superior while everyone waited.

Lavinia came beside them and touched Lady Tamworth's shoulder. "Reggie and Claudia, you must be *terribly* shaken. Anything I can do for you? Anything at all?"

Kat wondered: *Did Lavinia feel some responsibility for this robbery? The shooting?*

Her house, her driver.

So far, she didn't *seem* shaken. But Kat guessed that people of her rank, in this country, were masters of the art of dissembling.

"No – I just hope that the authorities can find the blighter!" Reggie said.

"*And* get our jewels back," Claudia added.

At which point, Timms turned back to everyone, his private consult with Constable Thomas over.

"The coroner is on his way. With another constable who will stay in the garden tonight. Now," he looked down at his pad, "perhaps a last question or two, and then I can leave you good people be."

"Of course," said Reggie. Then, as if an afterthought, "I say – you don't think I'll get into any trouble, will I? You know, for..."

Kat watched Timms close his notepad. "Oh, I very much doubt that, sir. Looks like a pretty clear case of robbery to me. And you did what any gentleman would do in the circumstances."

Reggie looked relieved. Kat saw Claudia take his hand and give it a squeeze.

The two of them were clearly both still in a state of shock.

And Kat thought: *Revolvers at the ready... Woe betide anyone who tries to steal from the English upper classes.*

That'll never end well.

AUNT LAVINIA HAD given orders to Benton and the staff to – at last – serve dinner. And though Harry was famished, he stayed back with Kat while his aunt saw to things.

"You okay, Kat? I mean, hardly the best example of quiet English country life."

"Well – take out the jewels and the m'lords and m'ladies – and it's pretty run of the mill for a Saturday night in the Bronx when I was growing up."

"I'll bet. And I imagine when you helped your dad at – what was it called again?"

"The Lucky Shamrock."

"Yes, I imagine you saw some of the seedier sides of life?"

"That I did. Did I ever tell you about that time that I personally ejected two drunks who were using the bar as a boxing ring?"

"Hmm. All that horseback riding in the park in New York too. Very physical. Came in handy, I bet?"

And he was glad to see Kat laugh at this. He often thought that – amidst all her other terrific attributes – it was her laugh that had really won him over.

Then Lavinia came back: "There. *All arranged.* I think the duck's a little dry, but the vegetables – well not much harm can come to boiled peas and carrots. And to be honest, after all the extra cocktails, and that rather lurid tale, I'm not sure this lot will notice."

She shot a look back to the dining room.

"Look, Harry," then more slowly, "and Katherine. Such a dreadful mess for you to walk into."

"Seen messes before, Aunt Lavinia."

"Yes. Well, I've asked the housekeeper to prepare a room for you. And one of the maids has found a change of clothes for you,

Katherine my dear. I do believe she's found you a pair of shoes too."

"Very kind of you, Lavinia," said Kat.

"Oh, they're just hand-me-downs, you know. But I'm sure they'll pass muster for tonight."

Harry caught his aunt's eye and smiled, then turned to Kat.

"If I know Aunt Lavinia those, um, hand-me-downs will be haute-couture from Paris."

"Pyjamas too, and all that," said Lavinia, ignoring him. "You get yourselves washed and brushed, then come down directly and eat."

Harry watched Kat smile. "That would be fantastic. It has been an incredibly long day."

"I'm sure. But one thing. Before I return to my guests…"

"Yes?"

"This robbery, the killing. My driver! And well, I've seen our local police in action…"

"He does have a note pad!" Harry said.

Lavinia gave that the smallest of smiles.

"I'm just afraid of where this may go. The other robber that they may, or may not, find. I fear that perhaps…"

"Someone on the staff is involved?" said Harry, finishing his aunt's sentence for her.

"Exactly. I can't imagine what that would do to the family name. Our… reputation."

Harry anticipated what she was about to say.

"You'd like me to look into things a bit? Stay on top of it?"

Lavinia reached out and grabbed Harry's hand. "Oh, Harry – would you?"

"And Kat as well." At that, Harry wasn't sure he had Lavinia's total agreement, but he leaned close to his aunt. "My wife can handle herself, you know. Out in Cairo, working for the State Department – it wasn't all organising champagne and canapés."

Harry decided it was best for now to omit mentioning her time helping her dad at The Lucky Shamrock Bar and Grill.

Lavinia nodded. And Harry was reminded of how much he cared for this woman, who had raised him after his parents died when he was a boy.

He would do anything for her.

"Yes. Certainly. Glad to help as well," Kat said.

"Good then, settled. Dinner in twenty minutes? And hopefully everyone will then make an early night of it."

And Lavinia turned, and went into the dining room where – from the clinks of glasses, and the sound of cutlery doing battle with Lavinia's china – the party had to some extent resumed.

Harry turned to Kat. "Twenty minutes eh? Think you can break your own record for getting dressed?"

"Show me the room and I'll be ready in ten. Can't promise how clean I'll be though."

"You're such a romantic, Kat," said Harry, taking her arm and leading her to the stairs.

"Play your cards right and I might even put some real effort in – maybe get all this straw out my hair."

A SHOT IN THE DARK

8.

A HUNT FOR THE SECOND MAN

KAT TURNED OUT the light of the side dressing room and walked into the expansive bedroom where Harry was sitting up in bed, reading some random book pulled from a nearby bookcase. She stood at the foot of the bed as he carried on reading.

The slightest rumble from her throat.

He finally looked up.

"Well, now *that* is a sight. Even more of a sight than that dress of Lavinia's you wore to dinner."

Lavinia's maid had left the pyjamas on the bed, but they certainly were not any style that Kat had worn before.

"Must say, Harry. Dressed in these, I feel like I'm in the Forbidden City and not Sussex."

"Yes, I suppose 'chinoiserie' is all the rage these days. And I must admit — you *do* look like you would fit in quite nicely in old Peking." Harry paused a moment. "And I also have to admit, altogether... fetching."

Kat reminded herself. *This is Lavinia's house — the floor full of guests. Still — this* was *their first night in what was to be their homeland...*

"Well, then," she said, taking a step closer, when there was a knock at the door.

And she watched Harry hop off the bed and hurry over to answer it.

"BENTON?" Harry said.

The butler stood at the door, holding a silver tray, two chiselled glasses, a soda syphon and a small silver container of ice.

Kat, resplendent in satiny swirls of red and green, came and stood beside him.

"Lady Lavinia, sir." He tilted his head towards the tray. "She asked that I bring you and Lady Mortimer two whiskies."

"Well, yes,' Harry said, opening the door all the way. "It *has* been that kind of day. And how thoughtful. You can, um, put the tray on the table by the window."

He looked at Kat. Then said: "My aunt *always* tends to the important things."

The tray placed, Benton came back.

"Will there be anything else, sir?"

And Harry had an idea. If his aunt wanted him to *look into things*… he'd best waste no time.

"In fact, there is. Could I," Harry walked to the door, and shut it, "trouble you with a few questions?"

He studied the butler's face to see if the man registered any surprise.

But, ever stoic, Benton simply said, "Of course, sir."

Harry shot Kat a glance. If they were doing this together, it would be good to have her by his side. After all, the United States had good reason to post her to embassies around the world. To use a phrase he'd learned from her: *She was one smart cookie – no doubt about that.*

KAT COULD GUESS what Harry was up to. When someone on the house's staff robs a guest – and is shot dead – might as well start talking with the person who actually *runs* the household.

"I've seen quite a few new faces on the staff tonight. This poor chap Coates for example. A recent addition?"

"Yes, m'lord. With the usual excellent recommendations from the agency, and references from previous employers." Benton sniffed, as if – Kat wondered – he perhaps felt the question reflected on him.

"How about the rest of the staff? Anyone else new?"

"I believe, m'lord, that Lady Lavinia's personal maid, Alice Comeley came while you were overseas. Then last year we took on a new housemaid, the girl Jenny. Rather young, but she's been good as gold."

Kat remembered the maid who'd obviously been crying earlier in the evening.

Was she perhaps… Jenny?

"Dear old Woodfine still at her post?" continued Harry.

"Mrs Woodfine continues in her role as housekeeper – oh yes. She took a short leave of absence when her husband passed on, but came back steady as ever. And the cook… McLeod… I believe you know him as well, sir?"

Harry grinned at that. "As much as anyone can know a Scottish cook who dislikes anything you can't put in a pot."

Kat thought she detected a hint of dislike on Benton's part at the mention of the cook's name.

"Mr Benton," Kat said. "The grounds outside. Must have a crew on that as well?"

"A '*crew*' m'lady?"

"Sorry – guess that's not the word you use? Team?"

"Ah, I see. Mr Grayer, the head gardener is in charge there. His under-gardener – he's reasonably new – a Mr Huntley. Young fellow, hired about a year ago."

"I saw a stable," Kat said.

"Yes, m'lady."

M'lady…

Still hard getting used to that.

"Huntley looks after that as well, and the horses. Comes up from town. The motor vehicles were in the charge of the late Mr Coates."

She saw that Harry had his eyes on her.

Surprised she started asking questions or…

No.

He was waiting for more.

But Kat felt that she'd better talk with her husband before diving further into the inner workings of the household.

And especially about the dead man.

"Well – could you please tell Lady Lavinia 'thank you' for the nightcap. Very welcome indeed."

And with what Kat thought was a fairly smooth dismissal on her part, especially carried out by a newcomer, Benton took the hint, did a slight bow of his head. "I will m'lady."

Then he turned back to the door.

And when the door was shut again, the two of them alone, she said: "How about you shoot some seltzer into those glasses and pop in a cube or two of ice?"

Harry grinned. "Seltzer? Ice? With a single malt? What blasphemy is this?"

"Hey, just remember – there's few wives in this country can mix a drink like yours truly. You should be grateful to have me."

"Oh, I am, *Lady Mortimer*."

THEY SAT AT the table by the bay window, the half-moon outside now high in the sky above the trees, throwing milky-white light on the front lawn.

Harry clinked his glass to Kat's.

"Rather generous pour, I must say," he said.

"If these are the house measures, count me in."

Harry smiled, then she watched as he stood and peered out of the window.

"What is it?" she said.

"Movement out there – caught my eye."

Kat stood up and joined him at the window.

"Ah – it's the policeman they put on duty," she said, nodding to where the constable could be seen, pacing the lawn.

"Lord and Lady Tamworth's room is just two down the corridor from us, you know," said Harry.

"So, this is close to the view Reggie had when he was shooting, hmm?"

"Not surprised he didn't know what he was firing at," said Harry. "Even with the moon out, it's a devil of a job to pick out anything."

He stepped back from the window, and she watched as he drew the curtains shut.

"What do you say we have another chat with Reggie and Claudia in their rooms tomorrow? Walk through what happened."

"You think it might trigger some memories? Things they left out?" she said.

"We certainly could use a better description of the chap that got away. Shame we didn't see him."

"I do believe I was rather more interested in taking cover," said Kat. "Though," she paused, remembering the figure at the window, the shots, "despite that, I mean, I *was* looking all around. I'm surprised I didn't spot him crossing the lawn."

"Maybe he kept close to the house?" said Harry. "We'll look for tracks tomorrow, in the daylight."

"Good idea."

She sat down again, and he joined her.

"Harry – you *do* realise that this time yesterday we were still in Dieppe?" she said. "Seems like a lifetime ago."

"Doesn't it? How was the drive by the way?"

"Piece of cake," said Kat. Then a grin. "Mostly. Save for the tunnels."

"I knew you'd be fine," said Harry, smiling and raising his glass. "Here's to us."

"To us."

Kat took a sip. The aroma was peaty. Not her usual beverage, but oh-so-welcome.

"Harry – I wanted to talk about tomorrow."

"Fire away. Oops. Bad choice of words. Go on, darling."

"We're here till Monday it seems."

"Afraid so."

"And your aunt did ask you to look into—"

"She asked *us*. We're together."

"Okay. *Us*. To look into Coates, the robbery, and try to find out who his accomplice is."

"Not much faith in the local police, I'm afraid."

A SHOT IN THE DARK

"Been thinking. You know, back in New York after the war, I worked a spell for that criminal attorney?"

"Ah – your *mentor*. Yes, I remember. The great Sean O'Driscoll. Gave you that last *push* to get you to go back to school."

"That he did. And also let me interview people, take depositions. What you did before – asking Benton about the staff?"

"Yes?"

"You're trying to figure out who we should talk to, about Coates. Correct?"

"On the nose so far. Go on."

"I assume that includes Benton as well. Though I imagine he'd be a tough nut to crack?"

"Benton? Oh yes, for sure. Definitely a *tough nut*."

She laughed at the way he said that. "But we should talk to all of them. Yes?"

"Absolutely. And sharpish. Who knows which one may have an idea about Coates's accomplice – or may even have been in on the robbery too."

"Right, OK. Here's my big question. I don't know much about the niceties of life in an English country house. So then, how do I do that?"

She watched Harry sip, savouring the drink as he took a moment to respond.

"HERE'S THE THING, Kat. If *I* question the staff, well, it's all 'Sir Harry this', and 'Sir Harry that'. Hard for me not to be nephew to Lady Lavinia."

"I can see that."

"But you, well, even though you *are* technically Lady Mortimer, I think people below stairs might talk more freely with you. Maybe while I talk to Reggie and Claudia."

"Makes sense. And what else?"

"We need to talk to the gardener and his... *crew*, hmm?" said Harry, smiling. "See if any of them noticed anything odd about our friend Mr Coates."

Kat laughed at that. Then felt immediately guilty.

A man did die here tonight.

"Meanwhile — our chance of finding out anything about the chap that got away? Slim to none, I'd say, without a description."

Kat nodded. "Least we can find out if there's anyone in the house who was involved."

"And — just a hunch — I rather fear there might be."

"So, your aunt is right to be worried?"

Harry paused — took another sip of whisky. "I think so. And we should be worried too. Ten thousand guineas? God — sum that size — brings out the worst in people."

Kat nodded. Hearing the warning tone in Harry's words.

This could be dangerous.

"Well, at least now we're not short of things to keep us busy over the weekend. And then Monday morning, bright and early — off to our new home."

"Finally!"

She watched Harry finish his glass.

"Appears I'm done here. And I think it might be time for us to turn in, hmm?"

Kat stood up, slowly getting used to the silky pyjamas with their brilliant swirls of colour.

"Now *that's* a great idea."

And she walked over to the bed, feeling more like she was staying in a mysterious, exciting hotel than her husband's ancestral home.

9.

ABOVE AND BELOW STAIRS

HARRY STOOD ON the gravel drive by the fountain and watched the convoy of police vehicles drive away.

Looking at the house now, it was hard to believe the dramatic events of last night had occurred.

But with the body removed, the flowerbeds searched and some of the jewellery recovered, the only vestige of the crime was the gouge in the ivy on the wall below the window where poor Coates had dragged the plant free as he fell to his death.

Before they drove away, Sergeant Timms had said there was a full alert out across the country for Coates's accomplice, and a warning had been sent to all the Channel ports.

If this was a professional job, then time was of the essence – and Harry feared they might already be too late.

He turned and walked back to the house.

It was going to be a busy day.

KAT HELPED HERSELF to scrambled eggs and bacon from the sideboard in the dining room, then poured a coffee and joined Reggie and Claudia at the table.

"Morning," she said.

"Morning Kat," said Reggie, surprisingly all smiles. "Jolly good breakfast – as ever at Mydworth Manor!"

Amazing to think the guy put a bullet in someone just twelve hours ago and now he's tucking into – what are they called – kippers? thought Kat.

She looked at Claudia, sitting next to him. The woman smiled wanly – then went back to picking at a thin piece of bare toast on her plate. Perhaps she was a bit more rattled?

"Kinda expected a full house," said Kat, looking at the empty places.

"Oh – all up early and out riding," said Reggie. "Lavinia made it very clear she didn't want the morning's schedule to change."

"Understandable," said Kat. "Not you two though?"

Reggie fired a look at his wife playing with her bit of toast. "Oh, we're not the riding types. Much prefer the Bentley. Hmm, darling?"

Claudia nodded, then the smallest and briefest of smiles.

She, at least, was definitely not over the shooting.

Then Reggie leaned forward a bit as if sharing a secret. "Think Lavinia also wanted her guests out of the way while the local constabulary cleared away the... ahem... mess."

"Right. Makes sense," Kat said.

"Morning all," came Harry's voice from the door. Kat turned and watched him enter, pour a cup of tea at the sideboard, and then come over and stand at her side.

"Hope you managed to get some sleep," Harry said to Reggie and his wife, taking a sip of tea.

He's so casual in these grand surroundings, thought Kat. *No intimidation whatsoever. What's the phrase? "To the manner born"?*

But then – this had been his home for so many years.

"A little," said Reggie, putting his hand on his wife's arm as if to steady her.

"Jolly good," said Harry. "I was wondering. Bit of a favour to ask you, Reggie old chap. You too, Claudia, I'm afraid."

"Fire away."

"Aunt Lavinia asked me to go through what happened with you – on her behalf. Get a first-hand account – without the police in the way, if you know what I mean?"

Reggie paused a moment. "Not sure I do, old chap," he said, with a quizzical smile. Kat thought she detected a caginess underneath the smooth reply.

"Well, here's the thing," said Harry, lowering his voice and looking round as if to check they would not be overheard, "she's rather concerned that one of the staff might be involved somehow, and she thinks I might be able to help you remember anything… suspicious."

"Ah, I see…" said Reggie. Then he turned to his wife. "Claudia, what you think my dear? You up to it?"

"If it helps catch that dreadful man. Yes, I'll do my best."

"After breakfast?" said Harry.

"Splendid," said Reggie. Then he folded his napkin and stood. Kat saw Claudia look at her unfinished cup of tea then obediently stand too.

"We'll be in our rooms. Just knock when you're ready."

"Will do," said Harry.

Then he produced a piece of paper from his pocket and handed it over to Reggie.

A SHOT IN THE DARK

"Oh – I saw Timms this morning. They've taken the jewellery they recovered back to the station for fingerprints. He asked me to give you this list of what they found – so you can confirm what's missing."

"Ah, good man," said Reggie, taking the list. "Need to do that for the insurance people as well."

Kat watched Reggie take his wife by the arm and lead her out of the dining room, leaving Kat and Harry alone.

"You ever make *me* rush my breakfast like he just did to his wife, I'll punch you, Harry Mortimer."

"Day I see *you* eat a breakfast that small, I'll take that punch."

He sat next to her and stole a piece of bacon from her plate.

"Hey! Lady's gotta eat. And in case you forgot already – I actually *am* a Lady now—"

She took back the piece of bacon, put it on her plate.

"So, you better watch out."

"Looking forward to it already," said Harry, grinning. "By the way – *love* the outfit. Very... what's the word?"

Kat looked down at the faded blouse and baggy slacks that Lavinia's maid had laid out for her.

"Yes, Harry," she said, fixing him with a cool stare. "What is the word?"

"Um... interesting?" he said, barely suppressing a smile. "Yes, that's it. Very... *interesting*."

"Careful, now."

"Actually – I do believe Lavinia used to wear an outfit *just* like that when she did her gardening."

Kat reached across, put her finger on his lips.

"Ah," said Harry, taking her hand. "Stop digging?"

"That's my advice."

"And, as ever, I shall take it."

He leaned forward and kissed her. "So, what's your plan this morning, Lady Mortimer?"

Kat took a sip of coffee. "While you do your posh interview upstairs, I'm going to talk to the real people below stairs."

"Perfect," said Harry. "Meet for elevenses? On the lawn?"

"Elevenses? Um – and *that* is?"

"Oh, sorry. Little mid-morning coffee or tea break. Usually taken around eleven, hence—"

"I might need a dictionary to settle in here."

Harry laughed. "*Most* of our words *are* the same, you know. Anyway – see you then?"

"It's a date."

He stood up, then leaned in, kissed her.

"Love you – really do," he said, sneakily taking the piece of bacon back and heading for the door. "Oh, and if you *do* fancy doing a spot of gardening give me a shout, I'll show you where the wheelbarrow's kept."

"You'll pay for that wisecrack," said Kat.

"Can't wait," he said, his voice echoing from the hallway, then he was gone.

HARRY TAPPED LIGHTLY on Lord and Lady Tamworth's bedroom door.

"Come in," came Reggie's voice.

Harry entered, shut the door behind him and looked around the room. It was one of the larger guest rooms – a big double bed, pair of tall windows, sofa, table, wash-stand. A door leading to a separate dressing room.

Reggie stood at the window. Claudia was seated on the sofa, still looking pale.

A SHOT IN THE DARK

"Good of you two to agree to this," said Harry. "Bit more confidential up here. No note-taking!"

"Absolutely," said Reggie, arms crossed behind his back. "By the way – wonderful to see you again, dear boy. Must be years."

"Ten at least," said Harry. "Just after things ended…"

Reggie nodded, though Harry didn't exactly know what his cousin did during the war.

Didn't seem much like the fighting type.

"And look at you now!" Reggie went on. "Hear you're at the FO? Quite a high-flyer."

"Oh, I don't know about that. Just doing a few days a week, consulting and all that."

"We *must* have a chat," said Reggie, leaning in conspiratorially. "Give me a bit of a steer on what's happening out East, hmm? Know what I mean? Malaya investments, don't you know? Tricky part of the world to figure out."

"Malaya? Not my area, Reggie," said Harry, surprised by Reggie's direct request. "Sorry, old chap."

"Oh? Really?" said Reggie, looking disappointed. "Ah well."

Harry watched him walk across the room, hand rubbing his brow.

"How can we help you?" said Claudia, breaking the silence. The voice flat.

Cutting to the chase, Harry thought.

"Right. Well, you can understand Aunt Lavinia's concern – about the staff?"

"Utterly," said Reggie, turning back. "You just ask away, old boy."

"Well. First – are there any servants in the house here you've ever come across before?"

"Not a soul," said Reggie, looking to Claudia, who nodded agreement.

"So, no chance of old grudges?"

"Good Lord, no."

"And you saw nobody behaving suspiciously after you arrived?"

Again, a look between them. Then Reggie spoke.

"Well, hmm. Not so much *suspiciously*. But actually, there is one thing I did remember this morning."

"Go on."

"That chap Coates? He helped the footman with our bags."

"Interesting," said Harry. "So, he came up here into your rooms, saw it all stowed?"

"Believe so."

"Unpacked, too?"

"No, I unpacked later," said Claudia. "The maid – the young one – she helped."

Harry nodded. "You didn't bring staff yourself?"

Again, Harry saw a look between them.

"Um, no," said Reggie. "We're, er, rather short-handed at the moment, still looking for a new valet – dashed hard to find good people these days, I'm afraid."

"And we had to let my own maid go," said Claudia. "Only last week."

"Oh, really?" said Harry. "Nothing to do with theft, I hope?"

"Um, no," said Reggie.

Harry waited for more explanation, but none came.

Interesting, he thought. *To lose one member of staff is a problem, but two…*

For people like this, a major calamity.

"What about this young maid who helped you when you arrived, Claudia? Trustworthy, you think?"

"Well, I hardly know her, but yes, she *seems* like a good girl. What's her name? Jenny, I believe. Polite. Helpful."

"And could she have seen where your jewellery was kept?" Harry watched carefully. An anxious look flickered across Claudia's face.

"Well... I..."

"Did she, Claudia?" asked Reggie.

"I don't want to get her into trouble," said Claudia. "But I suppose it's possible."

"Dear me," said Reggie. "I *knew* we should have put everything in the butler's safe, the minute we arrived."

"But you decided not to?" said Harry.

"My fault. Came down for drinks early, got distracted. No valet to remind me, you see. Looking forward to a cocktail, meeting everyone, socialising, you know."

Harry nodded.

Socialising.

And the jewels didn't get locked up.

Something not sitting right here, Harry thought.

But what?

KAT SAT OPPOSITE Mrs Woodfine in the housekeeper's office, sipping her third cup of tea that morning, notebook in front of her on the table.

The room was cosy but sparsely furnished. Through the glass panels behind the housekeeper, Kat could see the kitchen, cook and maids busy preparing for lunch.

Mrs Woodfine had seemed happy to talk, but so far she hadn't been able to tell Kat anything useful.

Apparently, Coates rarely came into the house, keeping to himself in his small rooms above the stable. And when he did, he spoke little of his previous positions or background.

"So, you didn't really have much of an opinion of the man?" said Kat.

"Ah well now, I didn't exactly say *that*."

Kat leaned forward, now interested: "Go on, please."

She saw Mrs Woodfine look over her shoulder as if perhaps the kitchen staff might hear, then: "He had an air about him – you know? A kind of *superior* air."

"Not so nice, then?"

"Exactly. I mean, I don't like to speak ill of the dead but..."

Kat leaned forward conspiratorially, encouraging.

"Took liberties with the maids, he did. That whole uniform thing. Leather boots, gloves – you know – called himself Lady Lavinia's *chauffeur*, no less."

"Kinda cocky – for a driver."

"Cocky? Yes, cocky, that's exactly the word." The housekeeper lowered her voice. "Even asked for a pay-rise!"

"Really?"

"Hardly here a month, and the money not good enough? I ask you."

Kat made a note in her book, then saw the housekeeper glance down anxiously at the pages.

"Don't worry, Mrs Woodfine," said Kat. "This is all confidential. But it may help catch the man who got away with the rest of the jewels."

"Oh, I do hope so."

"Anything else you remember? About Mr Coates?"

"Well, whenever we had guests, well, again he'd make himself just a bit too *familiar* with the ladies."

A SHOT IN THE DARK

"Hmm," said Kat. "And how exactly did he do that? Do you remember?"

"Oh, little things," said Mrs Woodfine. "Helping take bags to rooms; cleaning the car special, like; offering lifts into town; carrying shopping for them. All that... attention, you know?"

"Popular with the lady guests then?"

"Oh, for some, why yes. Good looking enough."

"What about here, below stairs? Did he have a sweetheart, you think? Anybody special?"

"I'm sure you know. With her ladyship – it's very clear that's not allowed. Not allowed at all."

Kat nodded, though she certainly didn't know the rules of an English country house.

"I understand, but we all know it happens, Mrs Woodfine. Human nature, yes?"

"I suppose so."

Kat could see the housekeeper had something to tell her. Something important.

It would need a nudge.

Time to take a gamble.

"Well, I guess we all know now, Mrs Woodfine, that Coates was a bad apple," Kat said. "And a charming one too, from the sound of it. You and me – we're wise enough to see through that. But I'm thinking, a young girl. A girl like Jenny. Easily swayed, no?"

"Oh," said Mrs Woodfine, looking shocked. "Then you know about her already then?"

Kat nodded – the gamble worked.

"Such a silly girl, she is. I *told* her not to get involved with him. *Warned* her."

"But she didn't listen?"

"In one ear, out the other."

"When did it start?"

"Barely a week or two after Coates arrived. Up until then, Jenny had a sweet spot for the under-gardener, Arthur, Arthur Huntley. Nice local boy. Proper cut up by it all, too, he is."

"So, you saw Coates and Jenny together a lot?"

"Tried to hide it from me and Mr Benton, they did. But I could tell. Thick as thieves they were, whispering and all," said Mrs Woodfine. Then she paused, as if she heard her own words: "Oh dear. What am I saying? The man's dead!"

What indeed, thought Kat, knowing who she needed to talk to next.

"Is Jenny here this morning?" she said. "I've not seen her."

"Her day off," said Mrs Woodfine. "Good thing too, all things considered. She'll be with her mother, in the town, I expect."

"Ah," said Kat. "Never mind. I'll talk to her tomorrow."

But Kat had no intention of waiting until tomorrow. As soon as she caught up with Harry – next stop Mydworth.

If Coates had help on the inside, Jenny the maid was now a prime suspect.

10.

SECRETS REVEALED

HARRY HELD THE Webley revolver – the weapon heavy in his hand.

Heavy too with memories.

Every time he'd taken off over the fields of Flanders back in '17, he'd carried this same weapon in his holster. Ready to defend himself if he crash-landed.

Or worse – take his own life if he was going down in flames.

Every pilot's nightmare.

"You served near the end, didn't you?" said Reggie.

Harry nodded. "RAF."

"Heard you had a pretty good war, my boy," continued Reggie, patting him on the shoulder. "You survived. Like me. Well done."

A good war? That wasn't how Harry remembered it. Six months of terrifying action – then another six months recuperating from his injuries after being shot down.

And then the call to work in Army Intelligence, leaving all his pals to carry on the work at the sharp end while he sat behind a desk sifting information, interrogating captured officers.

He released the catch on the revolver to check the rounds –
knowing already from the feel that the chambers were full.

"Always keep it loaded?" he asked.

"Better safe than sorry, right?" said Reggie.

Harry wrapped the gun in cloth again and handed it to Reggie,
who went over to the bedside cabinet, placed it in the top drawer.

"Would you mind – just curious really – showing me where you
were when you fired?" said Harry. "You must have acted fast."

Maybe Reggie's vanity would open him up?

And Harry watched as Reggie went to the door that connected
the bedroom to the dressing room.

"Well – right. I could hear Claudia was in trouble," said Reggie,
opening the door. "So, I stepped through smartish."

Harry followed him.

"Had my gun up already, of course. Chap number one was
already at the window, then – gone in a flash. I knew I couldn't get
a decent shot off – still trying to get the gist of what was going on,
you see."

Harry turned to Claudia. "Where were you, Claudia?"

He saw her hesitate. "Oh. I'm not sure. It was all so frightening.
Perhaps – right here?"

She pointed to one side of the room, then looked to Reggie.

"That's it," said Reggie. "I saw her, right down there. Coates,
you see, had pushed her. I think she fell. Dazed, of course. Then
Coates ran to the window."

Harry was silent, trying to form the picture. He knew how
difficult it was for witnesses to remember details.

"But you saw the jewels?" asked Harry.

"Damned right I did! Fellow had a proper *fistful*. Pockets
overflowing, too."

"So, is that when you shouted a warning?" asked Harry.

"Yes! Damn fool ignored me, even with a gun in my hand. Climbed up on the window... Turned..."

"And you shot him."

"Aimed plumb between the eyes," said Reggie. "Had to – damned thief!"

Harry mentally calculated the distance. Twenty feet.

"From, right about here?" said Harry.

Reggie nodded. "Fine shot, eh?"

"Extremely," said Harry.

Then he turned to Claudia.

"And where were the jewels kept, Claudia?"

He watched her walk over to a small chest, which was just visible under a tall wardrobe. She slid the chest out and opened it.

Harry could see the chest was now empty.

"I wonder," said Harry. "Did the two men seem to *know* where the jewels were hidden? I mean, did they go right to your case?"

"I don't *know*," said Claudia. "You see – I just walked in – and here they were."

"And they had the chest open?"

"On the table there. Sharing it out between them, I think."

"And when you entered?"

"The big one – grabbed me. Put his hand on my mouth. He pushed me over."

"Did either of them say anything?" said Harry. "Anything at all?"

"I think he said... the big one said... 'shut it, or else'. Something like that. I'm still in shock, you see. So hard to actually recall."

"I understand. But all this is so useful. I don't suppose you remember his accent?"

He watched her thinking, struggling to recall and then suddenly her eyes lit up. "Yes, yes! It was very *London*. You know? East End."

"Not an educated voice?"

"No, no – not at all. It was rough. Harsh. Horrible."

Harry saw her sway, a sob breaking her lips.

"There, there, my dear," said Reggie, stepping in and cradling his wife.

"Oh, Reggie. If you hadn't turned up – I daren't think what they would have done with me!"

"Never you fret my dear. You're always safe with me."

Reggie looked over to Harry as if glad that his protective stance was being well noticed.

But to Harry, well, it all seemed a bit *theatrical*.

Then Reggie turned. "I say, old man, think that's enough for now, don't you?"

Harry nodded.

"Of course," he said. "Everything we've discussed – it's all so very helpful. Must have been difficult for you both to relive it. So... thank you."

Reggie nodded, as Harry headed for the door, then out onto the landing, where he stopped.

He guessed he had what he needed, for now.

And he certainly knew more than he did over breakfast.

The second man wasn't a local.

Reggie was an extraordinarily good shot with a pistol. Barely a couple of seconds to get off the fatal shot.

And one more thing.

Which felt more like an instinct versus a fact.

Both Lord and Lady Tamworth were lying about something.

Question was – what?

KAT SAT ON A swing seat at the side of the house, sipping coffee, enjoying the warm morning sunshine, and swinging gently to and fro.

From where she sat, she could see the meadows she'd walked across the evening before. And through the trees to the other side – the spire of Mydworth church was just visible.

The town itself just half a mile away, it seemed.

How many times had she imagined what this first weekend in Mydworth would be like? A stroll around the town, exploring the small shops, lunch with Harry at a pub on the river, a lazy afternoon in the garden making plans for their future, then perhaps dinner out.

Instead – here she was planning a trip to interview a suspect in a jewel robbery!

No doubt which of the two versions she preferred.

And what was also troubling her: *seven shots.*

She'd definitely heard seven shots, not six.

She felt two warm hands close over her eyes from behind.

Harry.

"Penny for them," he said.

"I was thinking about those gunshots," she said.

"Funny," said Harry, joining her on the swing seat and putting an arm around her. "So was I."

"You first," she said.

"Reggie and Claudia. Just spoke to them. Got a funny feeling they're hiding something. In fact – I'm sure of it."

"But why? They're the victims."

"True, they are. But – I just don't buy Reggie's version of the shooting."

"And then there's that extra shot."

"Exactly," said Harry. "You said there was a big gap between the first shot and the others?"

"There was."

"I wonder. Perhaps Reggie *didn't* give a warning. Shot Coates point blank."

"Why would he do that?"

"Anger," said Harry. "Rush of blood. Might make sense."

"So now he's covering up?"

"Claudia, too. If it's true – it's a bad show. The police may not have picked up on it, but if they did, Reggie would be for the high jump."

"There we go again… 'high jump'?"

"Oh – *sorry*. Slang. Means you're about to get punished."

"Interesting. Yes, he may indeed. But there's nothing we can do, to find out one way or the other. Or is there?" said Kat.

She could see that Harry was upset by this. Always hating it so much if natural justice could not be served.

"Nothing at all," he said, shrugging. "Unless he owns up – and somehow I can't see Reggie doing that. So how about, let's try to learn what we can about this robbery. What did you find out?"

So, as they sat together in the swing seat drinking coffee, Kat told him about Coates's reputation and about Jenny the maid.

"SOUNDS LIKE Jenny's the key," said Harry, after he'd told Kat about the chest of jewels. "Maybe she knew about the robbery. Was an accomplice? That would make sense. You going to pay her a visit?"

"That's my plan. But also – I think we should take a look at Coates's room, over the stables."

"Good idea. I could do that while you go into town," said Harry. "But you know, to be honest…"

"And you English are always so *honest.*"

"I've rather missed you this morning. First full day in the old mother country, after all."

"Me too," said Kat. "So, shall we do it together?"

"Like two cops in a crime flick?"

"Long as I get to be the tough one."

"You have all the fun!" said Harry, laughing and standing up and making the seat rock. "What are we waiting for?"

And thinking: *Can a guy be any luckier than to be married to Kat Reilly?*

11.

THE UNDER-GARDENER

KAT SAW HARRY shake his head, smiling as they walked away from the small greenhouse tucked behind the manor house.

The gardener, Mr Grayer, had no compunction about giving Harry an enormous hug, all formality banished between these two.

I like him, Kat thought.

Harry looked over as they made their way around to the stables, to where Grayer had said they'd find the under-gardener, Huntley, tinkering with the old tractor, trying to get it to work.

"Grayer? Tell you, he had me doing all *sorts* of things when I was a boy," said Harry. "I know more about mulching and pruning than your average knight of the realm does, that's for sure."

Grayer, unfortunately, had offered no thoughts on Coates, only having seen him behind the wheel of Lady Lavinia's car.

"He certainly seemed happy you're back," said Kat.

"I *know.* He's at an age now he could stop working, and my aunt would provide for him. But that man there? I doubt he ever will."

As they got closer to the stables, Kat saw a few cars parked in rows, including one silver sedan that just might have been the biggest automobile she had ever seen.

A SHOT IN THE DARK

"Hey, is that Reggie and Claudia's car? Wow."

"Yes. A Bentley. Top of the line. Hmm…"

"What?"

"What do you mean: 'what'?"

"I do believe I just heard a 'hmm'."

"You did," Harry stopped by the Bentley. "Car like this? Not cheap."

"I can imagine."

"And, well, you would usually be travelling with your driver."

"And they didn't bring anyone with them?"

"Right."

"They *did* say they were having trouble filling positions."

"Maid, footman and now even their driver? That's a *lot* of trouble with the staff."

"You sensing something wrong there?"

"I don't know, Kat. Could be nothing. Just seems, well, a little odd. Anyway, stables ahead, let's see what the under-gardener thought of the late Mr Coates."

"HELL-LO?" Harry called, seeing just a pair of legs sticking out from under a small tractor.

Right now the stalls were empty, all of Lavinia's horses still out with the guests. Harry guessed she'd had to arrange for a few more to be brought over to accommodate the party.

He waited, Kat at his side, the sun cutting through the high windows above them, making motes of dust float in the still air.

Huntley finally squirmed out from under the tractor, screwdriver in one hand, a spanner in the other.

"Yes?" Huntley said.

Harry looked at Kat, and then back to the man with a smile.

"I'm Lady Lavinia's nephew. I wonder if we might have a little chat?"

The man didn't move for a moment as if processing the request.

Probably in the middle of some vital bit of automotive surgery, Harry thought.

Then Huntley put his tools down and pulled himself to an upright position.

"Harry Mortimer," Harry said, sticking out his hand.

Huntley wiped his blackened palms on the front of his overalls and shook hands.

"My wife, Lady Mortimer."

Huntley seemed confused. Was it the handshake, Harry wondered? Not exactly protocol with the staff. Or leaving the "Sir" out of his introduction?

Followed by the "Lady Mortimer", which Harry guessed Kat was still getting used to.

"H-how can I help you?" Huntley said. "Been trying to get this old thing running."

"You a mechanic too?"

"Not officially," said Huntley with a shrug. "Do what I can. Think it's past it though."

Harry nodded, took a breath.

"Well, we'd like to talk to you about Alfred Coates." Harry paused. "You know, the man who was shot and killed last night?"

And then – Huntley was perfectly quiet.

KAT HAD A thought as Harry began talking to the man.

The second man, Coates's accomplice, could be anyone.

Even this unlikely fellow.

She saw Harry frame his questions very lightly.

A SHOT IN THE DARK

"You knew Coates, of course?"

A nod. "I did. I mean, he was the driver. Sometimes needed help with the car. Fancied himself behind the wheel – but he didn't know *nuffin* about how you keep 'em running."

"I see."

From the way he spoke, it was clear Huntley did not like Alfred Coates.

"I wonder," Harry said, "did Coates ever do anything – or act – suspicious? Something that you might have seen, that made you – well – wonder about the chap?"

A quick headshake. But then it was as if Huntley caught himself.

"Hang on. Was one thing. He was always taking his time with the ladies, y'know. One of those types. From the day he turned up – all the time."

Huntley rubbed his chin. "I didn't like it."

Kat saw an opening for a different line of questioning.

"What about with the maid, Jenny? You ever see those two together?"

And at that Kat felt Huntley – only feet away – stiffen. He even clenched his fists.

"Oh yeah. Wasted no time there."

Kat noticed that Harry was waiting for her to carry on.

And despite the setting and the man's obvious anger, she had another rather unusual thought: *Doing all this with Harry is rather fun.*

"Were you... friends with Jenny? I mean, before Coates arrived?"

A scratch to the brow, and Huntley looked as if this might be a trick question.

He took a deep breath through his nostrils.

Hit a chord there, Kat thought.

"Before he came, me and Jenny got along just fine. Liked each other, you know. Talked about things."

"Talked about things?"

Huntley nodded. "What maybe we'd like to do someday. For her, getting out of service. For me, getting my own place – small holding."

Kat nodded, feeling some empathy for the man.

She said: "You mean, you and Jenny made plans? Together?"

"Well, sort of, you know. One step at a time. But then – *then*—"

Fists clenched again.

"That *bastid* showed up. And that was that." Huntley caught himself. "Sorry, m'lady."

Kat looked at Harry.

Guessing her husband thought the same thing. This man in front of them was no accomplice.

But also, between Huntley and Coates – there was clearly no love lost.

SILENCE FOR a few seconds, then Harry's voice, low, quiet, waiting for the man to become calm again.

"You know of anyone Coates might have been friends with? Maybe someone who could help him, you know, steal those jewels?"

But Huntley quickly shook his head. "Seemed to me like – 'cept for Jenny – he kept himself to himself. Can't say he had many friends. Not here at the house, anyway."

"You see," said Harry, "we're trying to get some hint about this *other* man who helped Coates, ran through the garden apparently, then vanished into—"

But now Huntley shook his head violently.

A SHOT IN THE DARK

"No," he said.

That stopped Harry, so Kat jumped in. "No... *what*, Mr Huntley?"

"Mr Grayer... he asked me to check the garden, the flower beds and all since someone had been through them. Bound to be a mess."

"And?" she said.

"No-one *ran* through those beds m'lady. I checked them all first thing this morning. Run through them, stamping down flowers, leaving big footprints? You'd see all that. But there was *nuffin*. Nuffin at all, I tell you."

Kat looked at Harry. *Well, that doesn't make any sense at all.*

Harry gave her a smile. Then he turned back to Huntley. "What if they'd run the other way – back into the house?"

"Not across the flower beds, you mean?" said Huntley, rubbing his chin. "Well. It's possible, I suppose. Could have slipped back into the house."

Kat watched Huntley thinking about this, working out the implications.

"Mr Huntley, I want to thank you for the information you've given us," said Harry. "I imagine you'll need to get back to your tinkering with the tractor."

Huntley looked back at the machine.

"Not sure it will do much good, sir."

Harry nodded. "I'm sure you'll do your best. One last thing. Coates had a room near here?"

Huntley nodded. "Yes. You have to go outside, to the back. There are stairs leading up to it, sits right above the stables."

"Thanks. We're going to take a look at it." He turned to Kat. "*Right*, then. And Mr Huntley, if you think of anything else that might be useful you just come and find us, okay?"

Huntley nodded as Harry turned, Kat beside him, and they walked out of the stables and headed to the rear of the building, to Coates's room.

12.

MORE REVELATIONS

COATES'S ROOM was up a small outside wooden staircase,
probably originally a storeroom or a hay loft, then converted to a
small living space for the driver.

Harry tried the doorknob, but the room was locked.

He turned to Kat, the two of them standing on the small – and
rickety – landing outside the door.

"Ah, too bad. Have to wait until Lavinia returns, see if she has
an extra key."

But he saw Kat grin. "Harry? Didn't they teach you *anything*
while you were bouncing around the Empire?"

And at that, Harry watched Kat reach behind her head, her
hair pulled back, and remove…

A black hairpin. She took a moment to open it, straighten it,
and then said: "Watch closely. You are about to learn something
very useful."

And he did lean down, watching as his wife stuck the hairpin
into the keyhole, and began twisting it left, right.

"You've done this before, I gather?" he said.

"Lots."

"Interesting. Not a skill I picked up in the service of His Majesty's Diplomatic Corps."

"Really? Turns out I needed to enter many a locked door on my postings."

"Good old American ingenuity?"

Then a *click*, and the door opened.

"That is *very* impressive," he said.

She smiled back. "I have a lot of things to teach you, Harry Mortimer."

"Oh, I bet you do," said Harry, as he held the door open for her to enter.

"RATHER A NOTHING of a room," Harry said, taking in the barely furnished space: a wardrobe, chest of drawers, single bed, some cupboards.

In an alcove, he saw a small sink and a gas ring with a kettle. Above it, some shelves lined with tins and jars.

And on one wall a black-leaded stove. He walked over to it, touched the metal – still warm.

He saw Kat had meanwhile gone to a small chest, opening drawers.

He watched as she pulled open the bottom drawer, searched; then the one above; and the one above that.

Searching the way a pro searches a room, he thought, rather liking the idea that his wife had another unexpected skill.

Kat never talked too much about exactly what work she used to do for the American Embassy, in the passports and visas division.

But he was beginning to suspect it wasn't *really* about passports at all.

So far, they still held their own country's secrets close.

A SHOT IN THE DARK

And Harry liked it that way.

"Some clothes, but not much," she said. "Like Coates barely lived here."

Harry pondered this, then went over to the bed, lifted the cover – and peered underneath.

Yes!

He reached in and dragged out a battered leather suitcase.

"Perhaps because he'd already packed for his getaway?" he said.

He put the case on the bed and opened it, as Kat came and stood by him.

Together they took out the clothes one by one, searched them and laid them carefully on the bed. Not much. Trousers, shirts, underwear, shoes…

But all smart. All quality. And no clues as to Coates's destination.

"Travelling light," said Kat, touching the shirt. "My guess is… somewhere warm."

"Agree."

Harry tipped the case upside down – nothing dropped out. He flipped it over and saw a handful of baggage stickers, mostly faded and torn, but some still legible.

"Certainly got around," he said.

He watched Kat inspect the stickers: "Paris. St Moritz. Istanbul. Biarritz. Quite the life. I mean, for just being chauffeur to the English aristocracy."

"Gives a chap expensive tastes," said Harry, untying a label from the handle and inspecting it. "Hotel Negresco," he read. "My favourite place on the Riviera."

"Can't wait for you to take me," said Kat.

"Oh, it's definitely on the list," said Harry with a wink.

He saw her turn and study the room again, her eyes moving restlessly across every surface.

Harry saw that she had grown quiet.

"What's wrong, Kat?"

"I don't know. Just, um, well… a feeling. That we're not *seeing* things."

Harry nodded at the spartan room. "Not much more to see, I'd say."

Kat nodded back, but then walked to the tiny kitchen corner and looked at the shelves. He watched as one by one she took the tins, opened them – and poured the contents into the sink.

Dried milk. Sugar. Then tea.

"Aha," she said – lifting a folded envelope from the dusty heap of tea leaves.

He walked over and joined her as she gently opened the envelope and took out the contents.

"A train ticket," she said, reading. "Or rather, a reservation. For one person. Overnight. Paris to Nice."

She handed the papers to Harry to inspect: "Le Train Bleu – next Friday."

"Coates on his own?" said Harry. "Either way, looks like he planned to slip back here with the jewels last night and wait it out until the storm blew over."

"Or until they called off the checks at the ports," he said, folding the papers and putting them in his jacket pocket.

"Clever," said Harry. "This was no spur of the moment robbery."

He looked around the room again, imagining Coates making his last careful plans. The man was clearly cunning – and meticulous. Tidy, too.

He walked to the end of the bed. Small end table, no drawers, tiny waste basket.

He looked in the wire basket – empty.

"You know what's missing?" he said to Kat.

He watched her think for a second – then she smiled.

"Papers," she said – and together they looked at the stove.

KAT CROUCHED CLOSE to Harry at the stove, a pile of blackened ash in front of them – the entire contents that they'd tipped out onto the hearth. Coates had clearly burnt every trace of his identity, every letter, payslip, communication.

"See anything?" said Harry, as Kat gently sifted the ash, seeking anything that hadn't been incinerated completely.

"Nothing," said Kat, the ash in her fingers just powder. "He did a good job."

She saw Harry reach into the stove, and lift out the bottom grate. Then he rolled up his sleeve and reached in again.

"Nobody's perfect," he said, grinning – and holding in his hand a crumpled, scorched, envelope which he passed to Kat, wiping his hands on a rag.

"Addressed to Coates, here at the manor house," he said.

Kat looked at the surviving fragment of writing on the front of the envelope. Just a few ink letters on the scorched paper, barely enough to decipher a hand.

Though the "C" of "Coates" had a distinctive curl to it – a flourish she made a mental note of.

She smoothed the burnt envelope flat, then opened it.

"And?"

"Empty."

Harry edged closer to her. "Let me have a look."

And Kat handed him the blackened envelope, turning it over on his hand.

"Can just make out a postmark," said Harry. "Dated a week ago. Salisbury."

"That far from here?"

Harry shook his head, as they both stood up. "Fifty miles or so."

"Could be important. Worth investigating – see what links Coates has to the place."

"True," said Harry. "Though the letter could have been posted anywhere within a five-or-so-mile circle of the city itself."

"Ah."

"And southern England, as you will learn, is dotted with little towns and villages that even their own residents haven't heard of."

And, at that, Kat laughed.

"You know, Harry – only an observation – but based on my interactions with your countrymen here, I do believe I may be the only person who gets your sense of humour."

"Oh really? Then you must stick close then," said Harry, handing the envelope back to her. "Can't have all my best lines going to waste."

Kat carefully slipped the burnt envelope into the pocket of her slacks.

"So this – outside of the postmark – tells us nothing. But the ticket, the suitcase… You know who we have to speak to."

Harry nodded. "Jenny. 'Fraid though, she might be a tad fragile."

"I know. And yet, she may know things about Coates, about the robbery."

"His accomplice."

"She might even be an accomplice herself, Harry. Given what Huntley said about those flowerbeds."

A SHOT IN THE DARK

He nodded: "When we're done with her, hopefully knowing more, my aunt and her guests should all be back from their little jaunt in the country. Oh – I had another idea."

"Yes?"

"I have a… *friend* in London. Chap can pretty much access any records. For anyone."

"Ohhh. A *powerful* friend."

"We help each other from time to time. Let me give him a quick call, see what he can learn about Coates."

"Coates had excellent references, Benton said."

"So he did," Harry said. "Anyway, I'll hurry to the house phone. Won't take but a minute."

"By the way, Mrs Woodfine told me that some of the house guests have decided to leave early tomorrow."

"Ah."

"Right after breakfast, I believe."

"So we have a little time pressure," Harry said.

"Think so."

"Let's get to it, then. The phone call, then we find Jenny. Besides, it's high time you actually saw the quite lovely little town of Mydworth."

13.

MARKET DAY

SINCE THE ALVIS was still at the Dower House, Harry suggested they walk into town, rather than get a lift from one of the staff.

A beautiful day, he had said, *why not enjoy it?*

One of the weekend guests had lent Kat a summer dress and some sandals, so she was happy to agree.

Not least to put an end to Harry's gardening jokes.

As they made their way down the long gravel drive through woodland, then across an open meadow dotted with oak trees, Kat listened as Harry talked about growing up and playing in these grounds.

At the end of the drive, a pair of tall stone pillars stood, massive gates open at each side.

Through the gates, and Kat saw they were right on a busy road: horses pulling carts, young lads pushing handcarts piled with produce, the occasional car and truck chugging past.

She hadn't realised how close Mydworth Manor was to the town – she could see a line of houses built right up against the southern walls of the estate, next to an imposing church.

"Not always as busy as this," said Harry, taking her hand as they crossed the road together. "Market day, you see."

Kat recognised the inn she'd driven past only the night before, now packed with Saturday visitors to the town.

"And this − right here − is what passes for the high street in Mydworth," said Harry, grinning and pointing to the narrow, cobbled street she'd driven up in the Alvis. "Number forty-eight, we're looking for. Should be down on the left."

No room for cars this morning, the lane bustling with shoppers and workers, children playing, the little stores all open, Kat and Harry having to thread their way through the crowd.

They soon found the house they were looking for, sandwiched between a dairy and a cobbler; the paint peeling, windows with old grey net for curtains. Kat knocked on the door and they waited. No response. She knocked again.

After some minutes, she heard a bolt slide and the door opened a few inches. A woman with a worn, tired face peered out at them.

Jenny's mother, guessed Kat. *Old before her time*, she thought.

Lots of work, not much joy, and maybe no husband in sight. Lost to the war perhaps?

The woman didn't invite them in. But though guarded and respectful, she told them that her daughter had gone to the square to buy yarn in the market.

Kat thanked her. Just as they left, the door almost closed again, the mother said: "She's not in any trouble, my Jenny, is she?"

Every mother's concern.

And Kat turned to her. A smile. Then, perhaps not with quite the confidence the mother would have liked, Kat said, "No, I don't think so."

Then it was off to the square.

"WELL, ISN'T *this* something," Kat said as they reached the bottom of the narrow, cobbled street and entered Market Square.

The scene – certainly nothing she had experienced in the Bronx, or even in the crowded lanes and market stalls of Istanbul or Cairo – was like something from another era completely.

Walking past a fishmonger, with his catch of cod, haddock and seabass – probably only hours old – sitting on beds of ice, melting, as the water dribbled down to the cobblestones below.

And giant cuts of beef, pork, chickens and even ducks suspended from another nearby stall. The portly butcher and what must have been his son, standing amidst the carnage, shiny knives ready to cut and wrap whatever sized piece desired. The man wore a dapper straw hat while his white apron had big splotches of blood red.

"This market," Kat said, "had to be this way hundreds of years ago, right?"

"Imagine so. Never really thought about it. Farmers; fisherman from Littlehampton; local vegetables, season by season."

"And all the handicrafts. They do this every Saturday?"

"Rain or shine. And, you know, at Christmas time, well, that's something *really* special. All the stalls decorated, a chill in the air. Jolly great tree over there in the corner. Carols. Mulled wine in the pub."

"Mulled wine? Now that's one cocktail I never had."

Harry took her hand. "Something for you – Lady Mortimer – to look forward to."

"I will."

She looked around the square, imagining this summer scene transformed by snow into some kind of Dickensian Christmas.

Towering above the square was what she guessed was the town hall, its large spire pointing to the sky. And midway up the spire, a golden clock face.

A SHOT IN THE DARK

But so far, no sign of Jenny.

"Think we missed her?" Harry said.

"Maybe. Let's keep walking – as for me, I'll try not to get distracted."

Kat had also noticed something else. When she spoke, people quickly turned and *looked*.

It wasn't anything she had experienced working in places like Berlin and Cairo, especially in the tight circle of diplomats where there was always a plethora of languages and accents.

But here…

Her American accent, tinged with a bit of Bronx, must be so unfamiliar to people. Even the American actors in the talkies spoke mostly with what must have sounded like a British accent of some kind.

Kat made a note. *Just by* talking, *I can create a bit of a stir.*

And if this is going to be my home, best I tread gently.

She thought of that novel she'd read in her first year of college: *A Connecticut Yankee in King Arthur's Court.*

Except – one thing Kat knew for sure – her home on 231st Street in the Bronx certainly was no Connecticut farm.

Then, as she walked with Harry, taking in the brilliant sight of all the stalls, really just enjoying it while she thought about how she'd have to adapt, to fit in – *she spotted someone.*

"Harry—" she said, touching his arm. "Over there, that stall with yarn. That's her."

"Why, so it is."

He turned to her. Without discussing it, she knew Harry was thinking that she should be the one to talk to the girl.

"You ready?"

Kat nodded. And they walked directly to Jenny, the young maid who perhaps had loved Coates.

Who perhaps had known what he had been planning all along. And perhaps had even been part of those plans herself.

A SHOT IN THE DARK

14.

THE TRUTH ABOUT ALFRED COATES

KAT TOUCHED THE girl's shoulder. She was carrying a bag full of items purchased in the market, the bushy green stems of a bunch of carrots sticking out at the very top.

Jenny spun around.

"Oh! Sir Harry... your ladyship... I um——"

Kat smiled. "Jenny, my husband and I were hoping we could talk to you."

Kat noticed Jenny's eyes dart right and left. And what had been a warm, near-medieval scene of people purchasing the freshest of wares, now seemed more sinister, as if they had just cornered the young girl.

Jenny chewed at her lower lip.

"Talk? 'Bout *what?*"

Kat took a breath. "Alfred Coates."

Now the hard bit...

"What you might know."

At that her eyes stopped darting, and landed on Kat's. Those eyes sad, resigned, as if the inevitable had just happened.

"Yes," she said, voice barely a whisper. "B-but not here. Somewhere quiet."

And Harry took a small step closer, his voice low.

"St Thomas's? Find a quiet pew, near the back?"

Kat reminded herself that Harry knew every part of this town. All of it new to her – but not for him.

Jenny nodded, and then – almost as if they were escorting a captured culprit – they all walked away from the lines of stalls, away from the square and back up the main street to the imposing stone church that overlooked the town.

HARRY LOOKED AROUND the church, the stained glass sending shafts of multicoloured light onto the rows of pews and the pulpit.

How many sermons had he listened to here as a boy?

And while he didn't think the rector's words had brought any real solace to him – not in those early years, when Lavinia had moved to the manor house to look after him – this place, the quiet, the deep rumble of the organ, the voices of the choir... all of *that* seemed to somehow make things better.

He knew that, in one of the side chapels, there was a plaque with just a few people's names on it... and his parents' names were there.

15 April, 1912.

That – he always tried to avoid looking at.

Turning to the right, he saw something new. A great slab of marble.

Etched in gold letters at the top, *"In Proud and Perpetual Remembrance of the brave men of Mydworth who gave their lives in the Great War 1914-1918. Lest We Forget."*

A SHOT IN THE DARK

For such a small town, so *many* names. Friends that Harry knew. Others, mere acquaintances.

On either side of that conflict, Harry knew, mere boys facing boys.

But not on a football or a cricket pitch.

In muddy, rat-filled ruts, carved deep into Flanders fields.

Harry ran his eyes slowly down the list of names, not skipping a single one.

Then he turned to see Kat, sitting close to Jenny. The church empty, just lines of small candles glowing up front.

Kat was taking her time. And Harry could easily see that she was good at this. All that time taking depositions for the lawyer back in New York, for sure.

But also, he wondered, *maybe the result of the mysterious work she used to do for the State Department?*

For now, Harry listened.

"JENNY…"

Harry saw that Kat said the word and let it hang there, a mere whisper in the quiet of the old church.

"We *know*. About you and Alfred."

The girl's lower lip trembled a bit. "Know. About—?"

"That you and Alfred were close, that maybe," Kat slid a hand on top of Jenny's, "you two were in love."

At this the girl only nodded. "I-I'm not in any trouble, am I? I mean, the police and all their questions?"

The answer to that, Harry thought, *will depend on exactly what Jenny says, or reveals, in the next few moments.*

Kat's response – perfect: "We're not the police, Jenny. We're just trying to help Lady Lavinia. To know everything that happened. You understand that, don't you?"

The girl nodded again.

And Harry was amazed to see Kat smile. That smile – devastating in so many good ways!

"Great. So – I need to ask you then – what *did* you know? About the robbery? About what Alfred planned?"

Jenny looked away; up to the front of the church; to the pulpit, the altar, the stained glass at the very front, now darkening with the sun slipping into the western sky.

She took a long time to respond.

But then the girl turned back. And the words came fast.

"WE HAD A PLAN, we did. I mean, I didn't want to have my mother's life. And him too. Neither of us wanted to stay like *this*, in service. He said he knew how to get out."

Harry slid a bit closer to Kat, wanting to catch every word. Curious, of course, but also tense with the thought: *This girl may tell us everything.*

"Out?" said Kat.

"Th-that's right. How to get both of us out."

"Did he say where? Was there a place he talked about going to?"

"A place? No. Just – *out*. Away."

Harry saw Kat glance over at him.

If Jenny was telling the truth, then she knew nothing about Coates and his single train reservation.

And that there never was a plan to go anywhere with this young girl.

A SHOT IN THE DARK

Poor kid had been lied to.

He watched Kat lean in close to Jenny again. "So, Jenny – did Alfred tell you *how* he was going to get you out?"

"He said, there were people coming to the house, people travelling with jewels. Rich people, people with *so* much, when we have nothing."

Harry had to ask something, even as Kat still held the girl's hand.

"He told you he planned on robbing someone?" Harry said. Jenny nodded.

"And so, you knew who he was going to rob?"

Another nod. "Lord and Lady Tamworth."

"He said how he planned to do it?"

"Yes... h-he said he would slip into their room, when everyone was down having their drinks, getting ready for dinner."

Another look from Kat, both of them being so careful.

"Am I in trouble now? Will the police find out, will I—?"

Harry saw Kat give the girl's small hand a squeeze. And then not answer that question.

"Jenny. I imagine," Kat said slowly, "that he must have asked *you* to find out where Lady Tamworth kept her jewels, that you—"

At that Jenny shook her head.

"No, not at all. He never asked me to do *anything*."

Interesting, thought Harry. *Actually... confusing.*

Not the answer he'd expected. A young maid, in and out of Reggie and Claudia's rooms would know *exactly* where to go for the jewels.

And yet, if she was telling the truth – and Harry now had no doubt that the frightened girl *was* telling the truth – it seemed Coates *didn't* ask for that help.

He let that odd revelation sink in.

KAT TOOK A MOMENT to work out what to ask next. She hadn't expected that answer – not at all.

Why would Coates not use her help, or need it?

For that, Kat could think of no reasonable answer. But there was one more area that she knew that they had to dive into.

"Jenny, I believe you. And that means, you know, you *didn't* help Mr Coates. You weren't part of the robbery."

The girl nodded at this, relief filling her face.

"Could have just been all talk, as far as you were concerned. But about that 'talk', there's one other thing I need to ask you."

A big moment here, something key to finding out what really happened the night before.

"There was another man who helped Alfred. A man who got away, taking most of the jewels."

Another pause, Jenny's eyes locked on hers.

"Did Alfred ever speak of this man; this accomplice?"

And now, oh-so-slowly Jenny shook her head.

"No. He just said he was going to do it. That it was all worked out. Kept saying that, he did. Nothing for me to worry about. It's all 'set', is what he said. But no mention of anyone else."

Kat felt Harry, who had been so still beside her, shift in his seat.

"Jenny," he said, "is it possible that Alfred had an accomplice all lined up, and never told you?"

The girl's face showed that she found the question incomprehensible.

"No, m'lord. Alfred told me *everything*. If there was someone else he would have said," she said firmly

"I'm sure he would, Jenny," said Kat, nodding.

"Is that all?" asked the girl. "Can I go? Mum will be wondering where I am."

"Just one last question," said Kat. "Did Alfred ever mention Salisbury to you?"

"Salisbury?" said Jenny, looking confused. "Why would he?"

"He never talked about going there? Or having friends there? Or near there?"

Jenny shook her head: "Salisbury's *miles* away!"

"It is," said Harry, smiling. "How about France? Did he ever talk about France?"

But Jenny just shook her head again and looked confused. Kat felt sure now that Coates hadn't planned on taking Jenny with him to the Riviera.

Whoever he'd imagined having on his arm on the promenade in Nice it clearly wasn't this country girl.

More likely poor Jenny was to be used if Coates needed help with the robbery. If he needed help getting into a room, learning where the jewels were kept, or even creating some kind of distraction.

In a word, the gullible girl was just – *insurance.*

Kat looked back to Harry. They couldn't interview the dead man, so all they knew was what Jenny was sharing. And she clearly knew nothing about the second man, the man from London's East End – or possibly Salisbury.

But if so, then there was another obvious question. *Were there other things that Alfred Coates didn't tell this girl?*

At that, the door to the church opened with a creak that echoed in the vaults. An elderly woman walked in, a bit of an unsteady wobble in her walk.

Wanting some quiet perhaps; a solitary prayer.

Kat looked at Harry and gave the girl's hand a final squeeze, signalling that the chat was over.

It was time to leave.

A SHOT IN THE DARK

15.

THE COCKTAIL HOUR

HARRY EASED THE Alvis through the gates of Mydworth
Manor and opened the throttle as they headed up the long gravel
drive across the open meadows.

They'd dropped in at the Dower House to pick up the car – Kat
desperate to have her luggage with her.

They hadn't lingered outside the house – both of them keen to
'arrive' in style, as they'd always planned.

And in truth – they had matters to talk about. Urgent matters.

He looked across at Kat who was staring out at the meadows,
fields dotted with sheep and the occasional deer straying from the
nearby woods.

She'd taken the clips out of her hair and it streamed and
billowed behind her in the wind.

So beautiful, he thought.

"So – investigator Reilly – what are you thinking?"

She turned to him: "I'm thinking, something here doesn't add
up."

"Go on."

"Start with Jenny. She telling the truth, you think?"

"Certainly seemed like it to me," said Harry.

"Me too. In which case – if she *didn't* help him, how *did* Coates know where the jewels were hidden?"

"He took their bags up to the room, remember?"

"True. But that must have been some lucky break if he just chanced upon the right bag. He couldn't rely on it happening. Or that the jewels wouldn't have been locked away, handed over to Benton."

"Okay," said Harry. "So, somebody helped him. Somebody else on the staff?"

"Yep. What I was thinking. Especially after what Huntley said about the flowerbeds. But if that's true, we don't have much time to find out who."

Harry slowed down as the drive turned away from the meadows and into the woods.

"You going to tell the police about the train ticket?" asked Kat.

"I'll give Timms a call, he can have the Paris train watched. But if the plan was to make the getaway on the Continent - maybe meeting up with his accomplice – I imagine Coates's pal will be long gone."

"And the jewels with him."

"That's right. I'm afraid we don't have much good news for Aunt Lavinia."

"We don't have much of any kind of news, Harry," said Kat. "Just a lot of mysteries."

"Not least the mystery of the seven bullets, hmm?"

"Ah, yes – that too."

They emerged from the woods and, ahead, Harry saw the manor house, glowing in the late afternoon sun. He drove past the front of the building, around the fountain and over to the stables, parking next to the line of guests' cars.

A SHOT IN THE DARK

It looked as if the riders were back: horses in the paddock, and a couple of stable boys from the town with brooms and pails of water cleaning up after the day's hack.

He and Kat climbed out, and Harry unloaded their suitcases. He looked up as Lavinia emerged from the stables, leading one of the big greys that Harry knew she loved to ride, its flanks still wet with sweat.

"Aha, my two 'detectives'" she said. "Solved the case yet?"

Harry smiled at that. "Not quite," he said.

He watched as Kat went over to the horse, reaching out confidently. The horse seeming instinctively to know that she was to be trusted.

"Oh, you ride?" said Lavinia to Kat.

"Whenever I can," said Kat.

"Wonderful," said Lavinia. "The trails here are superb."

"My boots and clothes are in the trunks – or I would have come with you today."

"We shall share riding stories tonight over dinner," said Lavinia. "Which is early by the way – turns out, some of our guests intend to leave at first light."

Then she turned to Harry: "I'll get Benton to deal with your bags. In the meantime, why don't you both help me with the mucking out and tell me where you've got to?"

KAT LAY BACK in the bath, the water so hot and deep it felt like that steamy hammam she'd visited back in the day with her pals from the Embassy in Istanbul.

Nothing beats a real Turkish bath!

Strictly women-only, of course, with massages inflicted on them all by a giantess with a missing sense of humour and arms like a butcher.

This bathroom though – their very own private suite off her dressing room – was so *very* English. The pipes had rattled and groaned as the scorching hot water – probably a rarity still for a lot of people in the area – finally spluttered forth in clouds of steam.

And the claw-footed bath looked like it had been in use since the time of the War of Independence.

Now though, filled with her familiar bubble bath and scents, it was absolutely the perfect antidote to an hour's muck-raking – and a frustrating day's investigations.

Harry had been called to the telephone and had been gone for ages – which gave her time before cocktails and dinner to review in her mind the whole case in the light of what Lavinia had said earlier in the stables.

"Poor old Reggie's on the ropes. Lost half his money on the tables last year – and pretty much the rest has now gone down the pan with all this trouble in Malaya. Afraid that losing the jewels will be the last straw."

It seemed that Reggie – an old Far East hand apparently – had massive investments in rubber plantations. The very plantations that Harry said were in really big trouble – and which probably weren't going to recover.

Taking a lot of City investors with them.

Like Harry, she'd sympathised when she heard this tale. But now, luxuriating beneath these scented bubbles, she'd begun to think differently about the case.

What if Coates wasn't the real brains behind the theft?

What if there was no "second man"?

After all, they'd found no sign of anyone running away below.

A SHOT IN THE DARK

And there was this: *Coates apparently needed no help in locating the jewels.*

So, what if the whole thing was a scam – maybe a con that went terribly wrong?

What if the affable, but broke and desperate Lord Tamworth – unimpeachable member of the English aristocracy – had planned the whole robbery so he could claim on the insurance?

Means, motive, opportunity.

Aren't those the rules of any crime? she thought.

That certainly had been the mantra of her mentor back in New York.

And Reggie hit the ticket on all three. He had the gun. He needed the cash. And he absolutely had the perfect set-up with the jewels unguarded, and a loyal wife who would back him up.

What if Reggie was the real villain of the piece?

All she and Harry had to do was figure his connection to Coates.

HARRY HUNG UP the receiver, made a final note in his pocket-book, slipped it into his jacket then sat back in the hall chair.

Whatever did people do before they invented the telephone? he thought.

Because these had been two very useful calls.

First, Sergeant Timms. Timms had been grateful for the information about the train ticket and promised to liaise with the French police and have stations across the country watched.

There was still no sign of the accomplice. Timms suspected the man was probably a professional thief. But all the relevant authorities were on the lookout and they were sure to catch him soon.

Harry's other call was a little more unorthodox – to a trusted source not available to the police: his old batman Alfie Withers.

Before the war, Alfie had done time in Pentonville Prison, the result – he swore - of a little "misunderstanding". And though he was now – for sure – on the straight and narrow, looking after Harry's London apartment, he still retained certain *privileges* as an "old lag".

The brotherhood of ex-cons.

Privileges that allowed him access to an intelligence network far superior even to the official one that Harry belonged to at the Foreign Office.

Alfie had spent the day digging into the background of the late Mr Alfred Coates and what he'd told Harry had been very interesting.

Very interesting indeed.

It seemed that Alfred had quite a reputation amongst the below stairs staff of the country's great estates.

Not a man to be trusted. Keep an eye on the silver. Watch out for your wives and daughters.

In the last five years, Coates had taken positions at four houses – barely lasting more than six months at each.

There were rumours of his "attitude" rife amongst the staff. And only last year he'd been "let go" by Lord and Lady Arbuthnot – the exact nature of his "offence" hushed up.

Yet somehow he always managed to escape with glowing references – nobody quite knew how. And he was always in demand – especially with employers that travelled to the Continent. It seemed Coates had excellent French, picked up as a driver on the General Staff in the war.

Nice work if you can get it, thought Harry. *Beats being at the sharp end where they're lobbing shells at you.*

Perhaps the Army was Reggie's connection to Coates? Had the two served together in France? Certainly possible. Much as Harry disliked war stories, he sensed Reggie would be happy to tell tales of glory if he steered conversation that way.

France, he thought. *Maybe there's a French connection here somewhere.*

He heard the clock striking in the library: six o'clock.

He looked across the hall into the main reception. Benton and his staff were preparing the room for drinks. Delicious smells were already rising from the kitchens – and he knew that all the guests would now be upstairs.

Just an hour to their early dinner.

And tomorrow, right after breakfast, Reggie and Claudia would depart.

He and Kat were running out of time.

"AH, THERE YOU ARE," said Kat, as Harry tapped on the dressing room door and entered.

"Wow," he said. "Whatever happened to the girl with the straw in her hair?"

Kat laughed. "That farmyard look is *so* passé," she said, turning so he could zip her dress, the black silk with diamanté straps that she knew he loved. "Now be a darling, won't you?"

She waited for that familiar gentle touch of his hand on her shoulder, then the slide of the zip – followed by a kiss on the back of her neck.

Always a thrill.

"There," he said, turning her round. "And may I say, madam, that you look absolutely exquisite tonight?"

"You may," said Kat. "And what kept you? I was having a lovely bath and I kinda imagined you might be back in time to share it?"

"Did you now?" said Harry, holding her waist. "You'll frighten the servants with these brash American ways, you know."

"Oh really?" she said, edging close so their noses just touched. "They don't seem to frighten you."

"Oh, I'm made of much sterner stuff."

"I expect you to prove that later."

"That's a promise," he said, kissing her, then stepping back and smiling, his eyes bright. "And I never break a promise."

"Good," she said. "Now you'd better hurry and get dressed – this girl's ready for cocktails."

She watched him cross to his wardrobe and take out his dinner jacket, shirt and studs.

"By the way," she said, sitting to watch him dress for dinner, *loving watching him dress for dinner.* "I've had some thoughts about the robbery."

"Me too," he said, taking off his jacket and then shirt. "You go first."

"What if there's *no* second man?" she said.

"Or rather," said Harry, "let me guess. Great minds, and all that. What if the second man is actually *Reggie?*"

"Exactly!" said Kat. "But Harry – what made you think that too?"

"Process of elimination," he said, popping the studs into his shirt, then walking over to her with his tie.

She stood and put the tie around his neck. "It was an insurance scam," she said.

"Precisely," said Harry. "But – here's the thing – somehow it went wrong."

A SHOT IN THE DARK

"Yes! Maybe Claudia wasn't supposed to go up to the room during cocktails."

"Right. So, Reggie had to chase after her."

"He found Coates and Claudia tussling," said Kat, making loops in the tie.

"Okay. So then, he shot Coates as he got away – couldn't afford to let him talk, reveal the whole game – that it?"

Kat nodded. "Then he grabs the rest of the jewels, shoves them in his pocket…" She took a breath, thinking all this through. "Claudia knew," she said, pulling the bows tight.

"Maybe," said Harry. "But maybe not. In the scuffle, she might not have seen Reggie do it."

"Reggie goes to the window, empties his gun, *invents* the accomplice…"

"Ah, no, wait," said Harry, adjusting the tie in front of the mirror, then turning. "Claudia said there were *two* of them – remember? Gave a description of the other fellow."

Kat thought about this. "Right. Okay then. How about, Reggie says to her – I don't know – something like 'just do what I tell you, and we can turn this to our advantage'? Not in so many words, of course. That work?"

"Hmm, maybe," said Harry, putting on his jacket. "In which case, she's part of the scam, but late to the party?"

"Last-minute invite, so to speak, but yes. Though, hang on—"

"Why the seven shots?"

"Exactly," said Kat. "Seven shots. And also – how does Reggie connect to Coates?"

"Aha! If we knew the answer to that we'd be home and dry. I did at least get the – think the expression your people use is 'lowdown'? – on Coates, and he does indeed have a rather chequered past."

"Your secret London contacts?"

"Something like that," said Harry. "Unfortunately, apart from that, all we have are theories."

"Right. So the plan for tonight – we talk to Reggie and Claudia, yes?"

"And hope they give something away."

"Not much of a plan, Harry, is it?"

"Nope – but it's all we've got," said Harry, buttoning his jacket. "More importantly, how do I look?"

"You're the handsomest man in the world," said Kat.

"And you're the *beautifullest* woman. Is that even a word?"

"Who cares?" And Kat leaned close for a kiss. "Enough with the compliments, let's go get a drink," she said, picking up her clutch bag and heading for the door.

"You bet your ass," said Harry, beating her to it, and holding the door open.

Kat laughed: "Your language these days is disgraceful Harry Mortimer."

"Only since I met you, Kat Reilly."

"*Lady Mortimer*, please," said Kat, taking his arm as they walked to the grand staircase together and went down to dinner.

A SHOT IN THE DARK

16.

A DINNER TO REMEMBER

HARRY DIDN'T HAVE to work hard to get Reggie's attention.
Lord Tamworth buttonholed him the second Benton had poured
him a Martini. He dragged him away from the other guests to a
quiet corner.

They stood by the open French windows, the early evening air
still warm, soft sunlight on the perfect lawn, the fountain on the
drive babbling.

And with Reggie properly lubricated, Harry hoped he'd soon
babble as well.

"Just wondering if you've picked up anything more on the
grapevine, old chap?" asked Reggie, his face creased in a frown.

"More?" said Harry innocently, though he knew what Reggie
was driving at.

"Malaya, dear boy, *Malaya*. Markets will open on Monday and
any inside knowledge might save me a pretty penny."

"Sorry, Reggie," said Harry, truthfully. "I know nothing more
than you do."

"Dammit. Shame. Spotted you on the old blower earlier,
thought you might be getting the latest insider stuff, you know?"

"As I said, not my theatre," said Harry. "Middle East, me. Out of interest though, Reggie – how did you get involved in that market anyway? Damned risky."

"Served out there in the war, old boy. Penang defences – for the duration."

"Ah. I thought, um… You were never in France, then?"

"Oh, no. Missed that dreadful show completely. Suspect I wouldn't have made it through – not many did – so probably a good thing."

Harry nodded.

Interesting. So, Reggie and Coates *didn't* share an Army connection. He looked across the room and saw Kat chatting to Lavinia and Claudia.

"Can I get you a top-up, Reggie?" he said, draining his glass.

"Capital idea. Come with you," said Reggie.

And Harry headed over to Benton and the drinks.

WHILE LAVINIA TALKED to Claudia about what she intended to wear at the State Dinner in the week, Kat sipped her Martini and watched the woman carefully.

The stress of the weekend's events had clearly taken their toll – there were dark rings under Lady Tamworth's eyes, presumably from lack of sleep.

But she clearly hadn't lost her enthusiasm for the great event. The only problem seemed to be what to wear.

"All three tiaras gone, of course, Lavinia. All of them."

"Dreadful," said Lavinia. "And those pieces that Coates had on him?"

"One or two of value, yes. But it was the other tray that had my real beauties. That's what I called them you know. *My beauties*. And my fortune!"

"That *awful* man Coates," said Lavinia. "I can't believe Benton didn't pick up what a cad he was."

"Please – you mustn't blame Benton," said Claudia. "Sergeant Timms said Coates and his associate were devilishly clever to plan the whole thing and get away with it."

"Guess at least you'll pick up on the insurance?" said Kat, seeing Harry heading over with Reggie to join them.

"Insurance?" said Claudia, reacting as if Kat had said something obscene.

"My dear Kat," said Lavinia. "Insurance can *never* compensate for the loss of a family heirloom. The history. The memories."

"Of course," said Kat, thinking that the only family heirloom she ever inherited was the pewter beer mug her grandfather brought from the Auld Country.

Good for drinking a cold beer, but that was about it.

"Still," said Harry, joining them, "it might go some way to softening the blow, eh, Reggie? Few thousand guineas?" Harry took a breath. "Maybe more than a few?"

Kat saw a brief look between Reggie and Claudia – a guarded look, as if both had agreed not to raise the subject.

"Yes, well, er," said Reggie, dropping his voice. "We'll still have to tighten our belts, you know."

"I'm sure it can't be that bad," said Lavinia.

"Have to cut down on the travel," said Reggie.

"Surely not!" said Lavinia. "But Claudia – all those delicious parties with the Murphys!"

"Gerald Murphy?" said Kat, surprised. Gerald and Sarah Murphy were an infamous Boston couple; immensely wealthy socialites who now lived in the South of France like royalty.

No shortage of cash there.

"You know him, my dear?" said Lavinia, an undisguised note of surprise in her voice.

"Not personally," said Kat.

"Me neither, Auntie," said Harry, now standing at her side and grinning. "But I wouldn't refuse a party invite from *that* pair. I hear they're setting the Riviera on fire."

"Anybody who's *anybody* drops by their place, you know," said Lavinia. "The fabulously wealthy and the amazingly talented. I really *must* get myself invited."

Kat saw Claudia shrug. "Sarah Murphy's a dear friend. Reggie and I spent last June with them."

"Really?" said Harry. "Where is their little place – remind me. Antibes, is it?"

"Yes," said Claudia.

"Not so little, either," said Reggie, grinning.

"Not that Reggie saw a great deal of it," said Claudia, smiling at the group as if Reggie wasn't there. "Preferred to head up the coast to Nice – isn't that right, darling?"

Kat was studying Harry.

He's directing the flow of this conversation, she thought.

And that was something to see.

"Hit the gaming tables there, eh Reggie?" said Harry, with a wink.

"Tables? Yes, well, might have dropped in once or twice to the odd casino. Just couldn't stand all that sunbathing nonsense. Sitting around drinking champagne with noisy American movie people."

"I'm with you there, Reggie," said Harry. "Love Nice anyway. Got any recommendations where to stay?"

"Hotel Negresco, of course," said Reggie. "You simply *must*. Is there anywhere else?"

"Then I 'must' indeed," said Harry looking straight at Kat and giving her the slightest of nods.

The Negresco, thought Kat, looking straight back at him. *Could that be the connection between Coates and Reggie?*

If so – well done, Harry!

All they had to do now was find out if Coates was there back in June and the police would do the rest.

She looked at Reggie. He seemed oblivious to the admission he'd just made.

If she and Harry were right – it was an admission not just of insurance fraud.

But of *murder*.

Before she could speak to Harry, she heard the sound of the gong from the hallway: Benton's announcement that dinner was ready.

"Shall we go in?" said Lavinia, and Kat saw her take Claudia's arm. "Let us attempt to forget the dreadful events of last night and at least have one convivial *normal* evening."

"I do hope so, Lavinia," said Claudia, and Kat followed them and the other guests as they walked towards the dining room.

"I meant to thank you for your kind words in the visitors' book, Claudia," said Lavinia. Then she turned to Kat and nodded towards the great leather-bound book that sat on a sideboard. "Do sign it too, won't you, my dear? A memento for us all of your first – and also unusual – visit to Mydworth Manor."

"Of course," said Kat, and she stepped aside from the group, walked over to the book and raised its heavy cover.

She leafed through the pages, recognising some of the names from previous visits: actors, writers, even minor royalty.

God, Lavinia certainly has held some star-studded weekend parties, she thought.

Finally – she reached the date for this weekend and read through the entries. Some – just one or two lines – others, more extensive.

Claudia's lines – the latter. A paragraph of lavish thanks, expressing a fervent hope that Lavinia would *"never, ever blame herself for what had happened"*.

A touching personal message, thought Kat.

But then – before she could reach for the pen that sat in an inkstand next to the book – she stopped dead, looking at…

The signature underneath the entry.

A single word: *Claudia.*

Written in a flowing, confident hand.

The C of Claudia with a distinctive curl to it.

The same flourish that she had seen on the front of the letter to Coates.

And beneath the name Claudia, the legend *Tamworth Hall, Sutton Combe, Salisbury.*

Salisbury.

The same as the postmark on the letter to Coates.

The envelope – the letter to Coates – had been written by Claudia!

No wonder Reggie was relaxed about mentioning The Negresco.

It meant absolutely nothing to him.

But Kat could guess that it meant plenty to Claudia. Somehow she and Coates had been together in the South of France.

Which meant – it was Claudia, not Reggie, behind the whole thing.

The robbery, the jewels.

And the missing tiaras? Well – maybe they weren't missing after all?

Maybe all along, Claudia still had them.

But there was only one way to prove it – by finding the jewels.

And only one opportunity to do so – *now*.

Kat stepped back from the address book and looked around. The reception room was empty. The guests had all gone through to dinner. Apart from her.

She tiptoed across the room, until she could just see through into the dining room. People were taking their seats. Footmen and maids were getting ready to serve the first course.

She saw Harry at the far end of the table, next to Reggie and Claudia: some instinct made him look up. She held up two fingers – and mouthed: "two minutes."

He looked confused – but nodded.

Then she slipped out of the room.

And headed upstairs to Lady Tamworth's dressing room.

17.

GETAWAY

KAT OPENED THE door to Lord and Lady Tamworth's bedroom, slipped inside, and quickly shut the door behind her.

She looked around: it was clear Reggie hadn't packed yet. Ten minutes ago, she would have wanted to start her search here, in this room.

But it wasn't Reggie's bags that interested her now.

She pushed open the door into the dressing room. There in a line – she saw Claudia's bags and trunks.

One or two stood open, with lids folded back. Others were shut, straps and belts in place.

Probably locked.

She went to the open bags first – and started to unpack them.

She didn't have much time.

HARRY SIPPED HIS Consommé Marsala – not badly done, considering it was prepared by a grumpy Scottish chef – and listened politely as the elderly artist opposite explained "the trouble with surrealism" to the whole gathering.

He looked down the table at Lavinia. She sat apparently engrossed, nodding and shaking her head at the appropriate moments.

The trouble with the English, he thought, *is that we're all too damned polite to interrupt.*

He knew that Kat certainly wouldn't have put up with this dull diatribe – she would have either loudly changed the subject or challenged the opinion.

If nothing else, to simply liven up the conversation.

"Where *is* Lady Mortimer?" said Claudia, next to him.

Woman must be a mind-reader, thought Harry.

"I've no idea," he said.

"She has been gone rather a long time."

"She has, hasn't she?" said Harry.

"Do you know where she went?"

Harry shrugged: "Up to our room, I imagine. I'm sure she'll be down shortly."

Two minutes, she had signalled. But two minutes to do what?

Harry didn't have a clue.

"I wonder if she's all right? She might have been taken ill, Harry."

"Hmm, now you mention it, it *is* rather odd."

He saw Claudia place her napkin on the table and slide her chair back.

"I'll just go and check," she said, smiling.

Harry nodded. "Thank you, Claudia. You're too kind."

He watched her go, thinking: *Something's not right here. Best to be alert.*

Claudia seemed worried.

But not about his Kat.

KAT EMPTIED THE last of the bags on the floor and sat back frustrated.

Nothing!

Three cases and three smaller bags – and not a trace of the jewels.

It didn't make any sense. She started to doubt her theory, despite the evidence that had been building.

No sense at all. Unless maybe Reggie was in on the whole scam too – and the jewels were hidden somewhere in his bags.

But she didn't believe that. Everything now pointed to Claudia acting alone – or rather – with Coates.

The two of them having some history together, and meeting up just months ago on the Riviera to plan this little heist.

That would explain how Coates *knew* where the jewels were hidden. The plan perhaps – he'd get half, she'd keep the other half, Reggie would get the insurance.

No losers in that little operation. Perfect.

Something had clearly gone wrong, but right now she couldn't quite figure out what. More important – she had to find the jewels before Claudia got suspicious.

She looked at the bags again.

What if the jewels were hidden in some kind of secret compartment? If so – it would most likely be in a new case, a specially constructed case.

She picked out the newest: shiny, white leather. Expensive looking. She lifted it up.

Heavy. In fact – heavier than she'd expected. Heavier than it should be?

But how to open up the sides?

She reached into the pile of clothes and pulled out a make-up case, opened it, tipped the contents onto the carpet.

Yes – a nail file – a sharp one at that.

If this was an error, Kat knew she would have some serious explaining to do.

She flipped the case upside down, ran the blade of the file around the interior. Silk, bonded to some kind of board. She tugged at the board until it came away.

Inside she could see another layer – but this was held in place by clips in the corners. Placing the blade under each clip, she levered until all the clips were open.

Then she lifted the layer – a thin metal sheet – and, as it came up and fell to one side, she saw… the jewels.

The missing jewels.

Tiaras, necklaces, bracelets, pressed tight in velvet recesses, sparkling and twinkling in the last rays of light from the setting sun through the window.

A stunning fortune. Ready to be secreted out of the house.

"Found what you're looking for?" came a woman's voice from behind her.

Kat knew it was Claudia.

"Not quite everything," said Kat without moving, her heart lurching. "I was expecting to see a gun, too."

"This one?" said Claudia.

Kat turned slowly, and stood up – to see Claudia at the dressing room door, a small single-shot pistol in her hand, pointing right at her.

"Right. Yup, that's the one," said Kat, with a bit of grin. Then turning serious. "The one *you* used to kill Coates."

"Oh. You worked that out?"

"I counted seven shots. You fired the first. Reggie just shot into the night. But one thing I don't get. Why kill Coates?"

"Silly boy," said Claudia. "He thought we were going to run away together."

"Oh yeah? Actually, I don't think you're quite right about that," said Kat. "Turns out he only booked a single ticket to Nice."

"Really?" said Claudia, picking up one of the smaller bags and throwing it over to Kat. "Well, what does it matter now? Put the jewels in there."

Kat picked up the pieces and dropped them into the bag, her eyes never leaving the outstretched pistol.

"You must realise – you won't get away with this," said Kat, handing over the bag.

"You can't stop me," said Claudia.

"Can't I? My guess: I don't think you'll shoot."

"Try me. Turn around and face the window."

Kat took a deep breath and turned, hoping, praying she was right.

She won't shoot? It'll be too loud, people will—
Or would she?

Kat felt a massive blow to her head, fell forward against the pile of clothes, and everything went black.

HARRY PUSHED BACK his chair and stood up. *Two minutes?* Kat had been gone too long.

Something definitely *was* up. He headed for the door into the reception room.

"Harry?" said Lavinia, as he passed. Silence now at the table, his hurried exit killing the conversation.

A SHOT IN THE DARK

Into the hallway now, and as he passed the corridor that led to the servants' quarters, he spotted someone running, heading towards the servants' entrance at the side of the house.

Lady Tamworth and she was running full-out.

What the hell was going on? Had something happened to Kat?

He turned and headed for the stairs, taking them two at a time, faster, faster, calling as he ran: "Kat! Kat!"

From upstairs not a sound.

He ran down the corridor into their bedroom – empty.

Then he heard the muffled slam of a window opening and a smash of glass. The sound – coming from another bedroom.

Out onto the landing now, running again, this time towards Reggie and Claudia's room – the main door wide open, but the door to the dressing room shut.

"Kat! Kat!"

"Harry!" came Kat's voice from inside the room.

Harry turned the handle, but the door was locked. He pushed hard. Hurled himself at the thing, but only bounced off, his shoulder in agony.

Then he remembered – Reggie's revolver.

He ran to the bedside cupboard, pulled out the drawer, grabbed the gun, turned to the door again.

"Kat! Get away from the door. Now. *Get away!*"

Then he pointed the gun at the lock and fired; the sound enormous in the room, enough to make his ears hiss; the smoky gunpowder smell so familiar.

He saw the lock had smashed – pushed against the door and, as it swung open, he looked around, desperately seeking Kat. But the room was empty!

"Kat! – what the hell?"

"Here! Out here!" came Kat's voice from the open window.

Harry ran over, stuck his head out – to see Kat climbing down the ivy, nearly at the bottom.

"What on *earth* are you doing?" he said to the top of her head.

"It was Claudia all along, not Reggie!" said Kat, not stopping.

Then he heard the sound of a car starting up – and he looked across to see the Tamworths' Bentley swing around the side of the house, the tail sliding on the gravel, then straightening up, heading past the house on its way to the drive and at the wheel…

Lady Tamworth herself.

Below, he saw Kat leap the last few feet from the ivy, land on the grass, roll over, then pick herself up and start to run – towards the Bentley, which even now was picking up speed.

And suddenly everything slotted into place, the tiny parts of the whole puzzle assembling, and he realised what Kat was about to do.

So dangerous.

But there was no time to stop her, only time to shout once more.

"Kat! Don't—"

And then, as he was dimly aware of others emerging from the house, shouting, pointing, the Bentley flashed past and he saw Kat – God! – take a great leap onto the car's running board, landing right next to the driver, actually causing the car to lurch to one side, then straighten up as Claudia grasped the wheel, trying to fend off his wife.

His amazing, fearless, beautiful wife.

But to no avail, as he saw Kat pull back her right arm and slam her fist square into Lady Tamworth's face. A fearsome upper-cut the like of which he'd rarely seen even in the most brutal of Army boxing bouts.

Kat's follow-through took her almost beyond Claudia and flying into the passenger seat.

A SHOT IN THE DARK

The Bentley swung around, gravel spraying – Claudia's head lolling back against the plush leather, the tail of the great car still making a tortured arc until it smashed hard into the fountain with an awful *crunch,* and came to a halt in a cloud of steam and smoke.

Harry watched, open-mouthed, barely believing what he'd just seen. Slowly becoming aware of Lavinia, Benton and Reggie now running across the gravel to the car.

And Kat raising herself up, standing tall on the running board, then stepping off and brushing herself down.

As if nothing remarkable had happened at all.

He watched as she walked gingerly back towards the house. Behind her, he could see everyone gathering around the car, dragging the stunned Claudia to her feet.

Kat stood below the window, rubbing her right hand, looking up at him.

"That there – you know, the leap, the right hook – was that entirely necessary, Kat, dear?" he said. "Seems – I don't know – *rather* risky?"

"That *woman,*" she said, pointing back towards the Bentley, "*hit* me. Back of my head. Knocked me out!"

"Ah," Harry said, grinning, "then you had ample reason. No further questions!"

Finally, Kat smiled back. "Nobody hits me and gets away with it."

"I can see that."

He stared at her.

"What are you doing up there anyway, in the bedroom?" she said.

"Right now? I'm admiring you."

"You can do that later. Right now, I need you to come down here and look after me. You know – give me a hug and a kiss, that sort of thing. Might even need a bandage!"

"On my way," said Harry, turning from the window and thinking, *If I'd known marriage to Kat was going to be like this, I'd have done it a damn sight sooner.*

18.

DRINKS ON THE TERRACE

KAT LEANED BACK on the cushions of the steamer chair and raised her Martini.

"Chin-chin," she said, looking at Harry who lay on his chair next to hers, sleeves rolled up, shirt open, panama tilted back on his head.

"Cheers," said Harry, leaning across to clink glasses. She watched him take a sip. "Bliss."

"You mean – this?" she said, nodding to the garden of the Dower House, the lawn soft and lush, the shrubs still in flower, the sun setting through apple and cherry trees, "or the Martini?"

"Both," said Harry. "Been waiting for exactly this moment for weeks."

"Me too," she said. She popped the olive from her cocktail in her mouth. "Better a couple of days late – than never."

"True," said Harry. "And there were a couple of moments this weekend when I thought you'd gone perhaps a *tad* too far."

She laughed. "Life would be so tedious if we never went too far, Harry."

"Well, yes. But that leap onto the car? And then the right hook? Ouch."

"That bang on my head? Ouch."

"Knocked any sense into you?"

"Doubt it."

"Good," he said, leaning over and resting his hand on her arm. "Wouldn't want you changing a thing."

"Don't intend to," she said, smiling.

She watched him take another sip of his Martini.

"Any news of Reggie and Claudia?"

"They're both being held in Chichester. Police have charged Claudia with murder."

"What about Reggie?"

"Obstructing justice."

"So, he really didn't have anything to do with it?" she said.

"Says when he saw that she'd shot Coates – he did what any decent husband would do. Took the blame."

"And he never suspected a thing? Amazing."

"Not the sharpest knife in the box, our Reggie. Seems he's rather neglected Claudia this last year or so. Abandoned her to go gambling in Nice – and she struck up a relationship with Coates there."

"Where he was chauffeur to some other guests?"

Harry nodded.

"Then, let me guess," said Kat, "soon as they got the invite to the State Dinner she saw the chance, made the plan, fired up Coates, let him do the dirty work."

"Then shot him when the job was done."

"*Very* nasty."

"Yes. 'Fraid she'll swing for it," said Harry.

A SHOT IN THE DARK

Kat shuddered at the thought. Then imagined Coates on that sleeper train south to the sun.

"Jenny was well out of it too then," she said. "She definitely didn't help Coates?"

"Seems she was telling the truth," said Harry. "Aunt Lavinia thinks she saw Coates doing a dry-run of the whole thing a week or so back – but definitely no sign of Jenny."

"Good. I'm glad. She's a sweet kid."

"She is – and being consoled by the under-gardener, so I hear."

"Ah, how fickle is young love," said Kat, draining her glass. "Hmm, Harry – I'm hungry."

"Me too," said Harry, putting down his glass and standing. "Maggie said that stew is ready – whenever we want it."

"Can't wait."

"Eat in – or out here?"

"Definitely out here," said Kat. "Let's eat, and drink wine and stay up until it's dark."

"Not too late," said Harry, giving her a kiss.

She laughed: "Oh no, not too late. We do have... some catching up to do..."

"And plenty of time for it too," he said. "Should be nice and quiet this week."

"Not *too* quiet, I hope," said Kat. "This last day or two – you know, it's been fun, hasn't it?"

"*Eventful*, that's for sure. Wouldn't want it every day."

"Of course. Your work in London? That's bound to be boring."

And at that, she saw Harry look over. With an amazing grin.

"Oh yes. That's *another* thing. Didn't have time to mention to you. Turns out that may not be quite as boring as—"

From inside the house came the loud ring of the telephone.

"Good Lord," said Harry. "Seems we're connected! At last! Wonder who that can be?"

Kat waited while he went inside the house to answer the call.

She looked around the garden, imagining her future here. All kinds of possible futures, events, experiences to come.

Seeing the garden full of people – friends, family, visitors – maybe children laughing, playing.

She and Harry growing older. Growing even closer.

"Well, there's a thing," said Harry, emerging again onto the terrace.

"Who was it?"

"The vicar," said Harry.

"Gosh," said Kat. "Only home a couple of days and they already want you back in the church choir?"

"Not quite, said Harry. "He wants us to pop over tomorrow. Have a chat."

"Me too?"

"Oh, especially you. Seems he's heard about our exploits – or rather, your exploits – up at the manor house. Wants to catch up with me too. But he has a problem, apparently. And he thinks we might be able to help."

"What kind of a problem?" said Kat.

"Didn't say. But he *did* say it was quite serious."

Kat looked at Harry, curious. He shrugged, clearly as baffled as she was.

"Okay. And what did you say to him, Harry?"

"Why I said we'd be over straight after breakfast."

She laughed. "Right answer."

He laughed too, then put his arm around her.

"Come on, let's get that stew. Can't deal with, um, all we may have to deal with on an empty stomach, now, can we?"

A SHOT IN THE DARK

And together they went into the Dower House.

What other surprises will the little town of Mydworth throw at us in the years to come? thought Kat.

I do like surprises.

NEXT IN THE SERIES:

A LITTLE NIGHT MURDER

MYDWORTH MYSTERIES

Matthew Costello & Neil Richards

A young poacher is found shot dead in the woods of a grand estate near Mydworth. A sad accident it would seem. But the boy's mother is convinced it is murder and when Harry and Kat investigate they find the poacher's life was not as innocent as he made out...

ABOUT THE AUTHORS

Co-authors Neil Richards (based in the UK) and Matthew Costello (based in the US), have been writing together since the mid-90s, creating innovative television, games and best-selling books. Together, they have worked on major projects for the BBC, PBS, Disney Channel, Sony, ABC, Eidos, and Nintendo to name but a few.

Their transatlantic collaboration led to the globally best-selling mystery series, *Cherringham*, which has also been a top-seller as audiobooks read by Neil Dudgeon.

Mydworth Mysteries is their brand new series, set in 1929 Sussex, England, which takes readers back to a world where solving crimes was more difficult — but also sometimes a lot more fun.

A SHOT IN THE DARK

Printed in the USA
CPSIA information can be obtained
at www.ICGtesting.com
LVHW091821070923
757245LV00012B/1279